# The Dragon's Call

www.rbooks.co.uk
www.bbc.co.uk/merlin

# The Dragon's Call

Text by Simon Forward

Based on the story by Julian Jones

BANTAM BOOKS

MERLIN: THE DRAGON'S CALL
A BANTAM BOOK 978 0 553 82109 3

First published in Great Britain by Bantam,
an imprint of Random House Children's Books
A Random House Group Company

This edition published 2009

1 3 5 7 9 10 8 6 4 2

The Random House Group Limited supports the Forest Stewardship Council
(FSC), the leading international forest certification organization. All our titles that
are printed on Greenpeace-approved FSC-certified paper carry the FSC logo.
Our paper procurement policy can be found at www.rbooks.co.uk/environment.

**Mixed Sources**
Product group from well-managed
forests and other controlled sources
www.fsc.org   Cert no. TT-COC-2139
© 1996 Forest Stewardship Council

Typeset in 12/18 Bembo by Falcon Oast Graphic Art Ltd.

Bantam Books are published by Random House Children's Books,
61–63 Uxbridge Road, London W5 5SA

www.**kids**at**randomhouse**.co.uk
www.**rbooks**.co.uk

Addresses for companies within The Random House Group Limited can
be found at: www.randomhouse.co.uk/offices.htm

THE RANDOM HOUSE GROUP Limited Reg. No. 954009

A CIP catalogue record for this book is available from the British Library.

Printed in the UK by CPI Mackays, Chatham, ME5 8TD

*With grateful thanks to Johnny Capps,*
*Julian Murphy, Polly Buckle, Rachel Knight,*
*Sarah Dollard, Jamie Munro, Pindy O'Brien,*
*Filiz Tosun, Anna Nettle and Rebecca Morris*

# Chapter One

Merlin paused for breath and looked out across the valley. He couldn't quite take it all in. There before him stood Camelot – the majestic citadel, its walls and turrets of white stone gleaming in the sunshine. Merlin felt a sudden rush of excitement. He was almost there.

He took one last look, then set off down the hill.

As he got nearer and nearer to the city, so the stream of people steadily increased. The bustling flow of traffic slowed Merlin's progress to barely more than a shuffle. By the time he reached the gatehouse, Merlin was almost at a standstill.

Merlin didn't mind, it gave him more time to look around. All the while his eyes darted from one new sight to another – colourful market traders, street performers and animals pulling carts laden with wares all jostled for space. Everything seemed new and exciting to

Merlin – with noise and colour at every turn. He wondered if it was always like this in Camelot, always so busy. This city was clearly nothing like the small village he had left behind.

'Oi! Watch where you're going, lad!' said a gruff voice behind him.

Merlin had barely felt the bump, but turned immediately to apologize.

'Sorry—' he began, but already the man was disappearing into the crowd.

For a moment disorientated, Merlin just stared at the retreating figure, before glancing upwards at the towers and battlements of the citadel and heading on his way once more.

Above the general noise of the crowd, he suddenly found he could hear the steady beat of drums and, curious, he decided to see what was happening. He passed through another gatehouse into the palace square: a grand cobblestoned courtyard encircled by high walls – and currently jam-packed with people.

Merlin stood on his toes and glimpsed a man with his head bowed, being led by two guards to the centre of the courtyard. The drum stopped beating as the procession halted below a prominent balcony. Almost as one the eyes of the crowd looked up towards the figure emerging onto the balcony. Merlin followed their gaze and for the first time in his life, he laid eyes on a king. The King of Camelot.

The crown was a big giveaway, of course. But there was also no mistaking the nobility of this commanding figure. Until this moment, Merlin had only seen those aristocratic features on coins, where the rather crudely fashioned profile had failed to do this man justice. Here in the flesh Merlin could see he had the bearing of a veteran warrior and the features of a powerful king. A number of other nobles, knights and courtiers were gathered about him, but Merlin's eyes were locked on the king.

'Let this serve as a lesson to you all,' said the king as he seemed to look at each and every one of the crowd in turn. 'This man, Thomas James Collins, is adjudged guilty of conspiring to use enchantments and magic.

'And pursuant to the Laws of Camelot, I, Uther Pendragon, have decreed that such practices are banned '

Suddenly, out of the corner of his eye, Merlin caught a glimpse of movement at a high window: a girl with flowing dark hair, blue dress and a pale face – her expression moody like a storm cloud. She paused for a moment, looking out at the scene before her.

But then the booming voice of the king pulled Merlin's attention back: 'I pride myself as a fair and just king, but for the crime of *sorcery*' – Uther allowed the word to settle like a weight on the crowd – 'there is but one sentence that I can pass. Take the prisoner forth!'

Immediately a loud drum roll sounded and everyone started leaning this way and that. Merlin saw the man drop out of sight, pushed to his knees by the guards. A muscular figure, his face masked in a hood, moved into view to stand over the man.

As the drum roll continued, the hooded executioner swung a large, fearsome axe high over his head. He held it there, poised in readiness. Merlin swallowed, thinking of the man kneeling under the arc of that blade. Waiting.

The executioner looked to Uther.

And Merlin saw the king's hand raised aloft. Then Uther let it fall.

The axe came down.

The drum roll had ceased a fraction too soon and the gasps of the crowd came just a second too late. All Merlin heard was the dull thud of the man's head hitting the ground. And without knowing why, he looked to the narrow window where the girl had been standing. She had gone.

A cold silence quickly descended over the square.

It was a silence only a king dared break.

'When I came to this land the kingdom was mired in chaos – but we changed all that. With your help the Dragons were defeated and magic was driven from the realm. So I declare this week a festival to celebrate twenty years of my reign – twenty years since the Great Dragon was captured and Camelot freed from the evil of sorcery!' He spread his arms wide. 'Let the celebrations begin!'

'*There is only one evil in this land!*'

The bitter screech tore across the square, silencing the crowd.

'And it is not *magic*! It is you! With your hatred and your ignorance!'

An old woman now stood in a newly empty space at the heart of the courtyard. As soon as people clapped eyes on her, they recoiled further. Something more than age had carved its marks into this woman's features. Her skin was deeply lined like bark, her hair as white as frost. Her withered figure was clothed in a shamble of rags and old blankets. Merlin thought he saw tears welling in the corners of her sunken eyes.

Guards were pushing forward through the ring of people now, but she paid them no heed. Instead she aimed an accusatory, crooked finger up at the king, and in a cracked voice cried out, 'You took my son and I warn you – before these celebrations are over, you will share my tears! An eye for an eye, a tooth for a tooth . . . *a son for a son!*'

Uther glared down at her. He had heard more than enough. 'Guards, seize her!'

The old woman spared her pursuers the most fleeting of glances, whilst grasping a pendant at her neck. Lifting it close to her lips, she appeared to whisper some hurried message to the stone.

Suddenly the air in the courtyard exploded into a whirlwind, churning up dirt and straw and driving the crowd back. The guards held their ground, but couldn't move forward into the storm. The winds seemed to be tearing at the old woman's ragged clothing, sending tattered ribbons of fabric spiralling up and up . . .

. . . into nothing.

The winds died as swiftly as they had begun and the dirt and debris floated slowly back to earth. There was nothing left of the woman.

A frightened murmur began to rise from the crowd as Uther turned in disgust and strode back into the palace. Of everyone gathered in the square, Merlin had not only heard the old woman's magic, he had *felt* it too, and now he began to feel afraid.

Around him, the guards had started clearing the crowds from the square. Although they were trained soldiers, a few of them looked as scared as the people they were ushering away. Most, though, were scanning the faces in the crowd, ready to arrest or kill anyone who so much as looked suspicious. Merlin thought he'd best be on his way.

# Chapter Two

Ducking in under an archway leading off the marketplace, Merlin found himself facing two impassive palace guards.

He hoped there was a chance they would help him find Gaius's chambers. And having politely asked the guards for directions, the one nearest Merlin jerked his thumb towards the stairs that rose behind him.

Merlin thanked the guard and took the steps two at a time, eager now to reach Gaius's rooms. He hoped they wouldn't be too far from the main palace – he thought the court physician would probably be within easy reach of his most important patients.

At the top of the stairs, Merlin followed a short passage which ended with a wooden door labelled *Court Physician*. As he reached out to knock on the door, Merlin felt both excited and nervous.

There was no answer, but the door creaked quietly ajar.

He peered through the gap. 'Hello?' he called. There was no reply.

Not sure what else to do, Merlin glanced left and right along the passage, before gently pushing the door open and stepping inside.

No signs of life.

He looked around the room, but still couldn't see any movement. There was, however, a bewildering assortment of glass flasks, instruments of brass and copper on every bench top. And lots of books: volumes large and small, open on the tables, stacked on the floor or crammed into shelves lining the walls. Dust spiralled in the afternoon sunlight, swirling in the air before settling on the jumble of objects before him.

Suddenly to his left Merlin heard a creak – he turned and looked up towards a balcony to see a figure balancing on a rickety ladder that was propped against some shelves. The figure was leaning precariously, with one arm stretched out trying to reach a book from a shelf high up among the rafters. Merlin had never met Gaius, but assumed this must be the court physician.

Not sure how to attract his attention, Merlin coughed, 'Eh – hmm?'

Startled, the man spun round and toppled from his perch.

There was no time for thought, just for action. Merlin concentrated all his energy on the falling figure and as a familiar heat rose through his body, suddenly Merlin's eyes glowed with a golden light. Magic flowed from his fingers out towards the falling man, instantly slowing his descent so that he seemed to hang suspended in the air momentarily.

At the same time Merlin focused on the bed in the corner, causing it to slide across the room to where it was needed. As soon as the bed was in place, Merlin's fire subsided and time raced on. The old man landed on the mattress, sending up clouds of dust. He lay there, a mess of brown robes and silver hair, stunned or physically winded for a moment, before rolling over and fixing Merlin with a hawk-like stare.

'How the devil . . . !' the old man exclaimed, glancing at the corner where the bed had been. He struggled to his feet and then turned to stare at Merlin. 'What did you just do?'

Merlin took a step back. 'Uh . . .'

'Tell me.'

'I – don't know.'

The old fellow shook his head and pointed at the young warlock. 'If anyone had seen that . . .'

Merlin didn't need to be told what would happen if someone loyal to Uther had seen what he'd just done: unbidden, an image of the executioner's axe blade flashed into his mind. His imagination unhelpfully filled in what the crowd had prevented him from seeing.

'It was nothing to do with me,' he protested. 'It was . . .' He racked his brains searching desperately for some reasonable explanation.

'I know what it was,' insisted the old man. 'I want to know where you learned how to do it.'

Merlin shrugged. Why couldn't he just let it go? 'Nowhere.'

'Then how is it you know magic?'

Hearing the word said out loud almost threw Merlin off-guard. Almost. 'I don't,' he muttered.

'Where did you study? Answer me.'

Now Merlin really felt a guilty heat in his cheeks. It felt so wrong to be lying to this man: the light in those old eyes may have been stern, but it was honest.

'I've never studied magic or—'

The man advanced. 'You're lying to me, boy.'

'What am I supposed to say?'

'The truth!' Gaius hurled the words at Merlin.

Clearly there was no hiding it from him. Merlin would just have to own up and face the music. Merlin knew he'd been right to save the old man and now he knew there was no concealing the truth – the old physician had seen what had happened with his own eyes. He hoped Gaius would show him some under-standing.

'I was born like this. It's been with me since—'

'Impossible!' Then the man seemed to pounce on another thought. 'Who are you?'

Merlin quickly pulled his bag off his shoulder and delved into it, glad to be off the subject of magic and on to the simpler question of introductions. 'I have this letter.'

He presented the parchment. The old man accepted it, glanced it over once – then admitted, 'I don't have my glasses.'

'I'm Merlin.'

A moment's pause and then the old eyes softened. 'Hunith's son?'

'Yes.'

Gaius frowned. 'But you're not meant to be here until Wednesday.'

Merlin felt bad contradicting Gaius, but couldn't think of a nicer way of stating the obvious. 'It *is* Wednesday.'

Gaius looked puzzled, as though consulting some internal calendar. 'So it is. Well, all right then. You'd best put your things up there.'

He waved to an unpromising door up three short steps at the far end of the room.

Merlin nodded gratefully and walked towards his new room. He came to a stop halfway there though, troubled by the idea that guards might come for him in the night.

'You won't say anything, will you? About the . . .' His eyes shot to the mattress. He didn't feel like saying 'magic'.

'No.'

Merlin breathed a sigh of relief. He turned.

'Although, Merlin . . .'

He froze in his tracks and faced Gaius slowly.

'I should say thank you.' Gaius smiled.

Merlin answered with a smile of his own. Then headed for his new quarters.

Gaius was accustomed to working late and often burned the candle at both ends. But tonight he stayed up later than usual fretting about his new charge. Having read Merlin's mother's letter, Gaius had a great deal to think about.

In the flickering candlelight, he pored over the letter a second time, digesting what Hunith had to say:

*It is every mother's fate to think her child is special, and yet I would give my life that Merlin were not so.*

*Ours is a small village and he is so clearly at odds with people here that if he were to remain I fear what would become of him.*

*He needs a hand to hold, a voice to guide, someone who might help him find a purpose for his gifts. I beg you, if you understand a mother's love for her son, keep him safe. And may God save you both.*

Gaius laid the parchment on the desk with a sigh. Troubled, he turned his gaze towards the garret room. He trusted his new 'apprentice' was sleeping soundly.

After another moment's thought, he snuffed out his candle, ready to continue thinking in bed. The future was uncertain territory at the best of times, but he was reasonably sure he wouldn't be getting much sleep tonight.

★

Merlin had turned in early, exhausted from the journey and the day's events. But by the time he had settled into his new quarters and unpacked his few belongings, the feelings of fatigue were swiftly overtaken by excitement.

No matter what else had occurred, he was here in Camelot.

Tossing aside his empty pack, he went and stood by the window. Taking a deep breath of night air, he stared out across the rooftops, marvelling at the size of the city before him. Full of excitement, Merlin felt that this must be the beginning of a great adventure.

Smiling, he turned away from the window and threw himself onto his bed. With his head on the pillow and his eyes drooping with tiredness, he saw Camelot stretching out before him in his mind's eye.

At some point, sleep eventually claimed him, drawing him down and down into darkness. And in that darkness a voice called to him through the stones of Camelot.

*Merlin!*

# Chapter Three

Morgana, the king's ward, stood gazing down at the now-empty square. This was the very window through which she had seen a man led to his death earlier in the day. To Morgana the gleaming axe blade, now put to bed in the executioner's block, was as awful a sight as it had been in the cold light of day.

The sun could bathe the scene in gold tomorrow, but the cobbles would still be stained with that one act. If only the memories were washed away as easily as the blood. Morgana would not forget.

She winced, remembering the pain evident in that old woman's cries.

Of course, it seemed as though others could just cast these things aside and carry on as normal. Others could sentence a man to death in the afternoon and dine heartily the same evening. Morgana could hear the music floating up from the great hall – lively ditties, to which some people were probably dancing. The pipes and lutes were accompanied by sporadic roars of laughter.

Then the music was joined by footsteps in the passage behind her. There was no mistaking the power of that stride. Morgana straightened her shoulders, but her eyes remained fixed on the axe and the recently scrubbed cobblestones.

'Morgana?'

Morgana turned, determined Uther should see the accusation in her eyes. 'Yes?'

'What are you doing here? Why have you not joined us at the feast?' the king demanded. His gaze, as usual, was like steel. Morgana stepped to the side of the window, affording Uther a clear view of the square, if he dared take a look.

'I just don't think that chopping someone's head off is cause for celebration.' Again, she saw the old woman in her mind's eye. 'That poor mother.' She didn't suppose it had ever occurred to Uther that condemned men had mothers.

Uther didn't appear to be moved, unable to see beyond the crime that had been committed. 'It is only justice for what he did.'

'Justice? For whom? He practised some magic. He didn't harm anyone.'

There was an angry glint in Uther's eyes: a hint of the iron which lay beneath his seemingly calm exterior. 'You weren't around twenty years ago, you don't know what it was like.'

History. The man was obsessed. 'How long are you going to keep punishing people for what happened then?'

Candlelight flickered across the king's face. 'Until they realize that magic has no place in my kingdom.' He spun on his heels, his cloak swishing imperiously as he marched off, closing the conversation. 'You *will* be with me to meet Lady Helen tomorrow.'

'I've told you I want no part of these celebrations,' Morgana called after him.

Uther stopped and faced the young woman. 'As my ward, I expect you to do as I ask. If you show me no respect, at least respect our finest singer.'

He turned again and went on his way. *Finest singer.* What manner of fine songs would Lady Helen of Mora sing, Morgana wondered, if she had been forced to witness the death of that poor man? In fact, Morgana had been looking forward to Lady Helen's performance – her songs and her voice were indeed beautiful. In truth, she felt that perhaps she could use some cheering up after today's sorry event and Lady Helen's visit might prove just the remedy, but she wasn't about to admit that to Uther.

She glared at the king's retreating back.

'The more brutal you are, the more enemies you'll create!'

He didn't break his stride, giving no indication he had heard her. Uther commanded her to sit and listen to singers, but he was deaf to anything that truly mattered.

She cast her gaze back to the window and the night beyond. She could no more change the man Uther was than the moon could erase what had happened down there in the courtyard.

The moonlight made little impression through the thick forest canopy, which suited the old woman well as she watched from the shadows.

A small cluster of tents stood in a clearing surrounded by campfires. Guards patrolled a short distance from the crackling warmth of the flames, unaware of the intruder in the undergrowth. Slowly, the old woman stole in towards the camp, using dark magic to mask her movements.

★

The fires cast distracting shadows onto the walls of the tent, projecting the movements of the guards outside. Lady Helen tried to ignore them. It had been the same on the two previous nights they had been obliged to make camp on their way from Mora. Uther's hospitality would make the journey worthwhile, but no matter how charming the old warrior was he couldn't make the road to Camelot any shorter.

She sang softly, entertaining herself while she sat at her dressing table, braiding her long dark hair. Lady Helen had half expected she would miss her maids by now: she had insisted they remain behind, knowing full well how positively crowded by servants she had been on her last visit to Uther's court. Uther always looked after her so well.

In the quiet of the night, she found attending to her hair a rather relaxing ritual before bedtime. It helped ease the nerves she felt at camping in the wilderness, but she would always be much happier with a roof over her head and stone walls around her.

The candles flickered suddenly. Lady Helen looked quickly to the tent flap. It was still closed and there had been only a gentle breeze when she had retired for the night.

Then there came the crunch of twigs underfoot.

Lady Helen's throat felt as dry as autumn leaves. 'Hello?'

Silence. She watched as a silhouette moved across the canvas screen like a phantom.

'Gregory?' she asked tentatively. It had to be Gregory, her captain of the guards.

After a pause, the tent flap lifted.

Gregory poked his head inside. 'Yes, my lady.'

'Is all well?' Lady Helen certainly felt better seeing Gregory's rugged face and his sturdy shoulders, but she still wanted to hear that nothing was amiss in the camp.

'Yes, ma'am. With luck we should reach Camelot late tomorrow.'

'That's good.' Lady Helen felt relief that the journey was almost over, but her nerves refused to dissipate altogether. Gregory hovered in the entrance in case his mistress should have any further concerns, but Lady Helen could think of nothing more to say and although his presence calmed her, the longer she detained him over senseless fears, the more foolish she would feel. Gregory must have picked up on it. 'I will be outside if you need me,' he assured her.

Dear, dependable Gregory. How could she feel anything but safe with him on guard? She rewarded him with a smile. Gregory ducked back outside. Lady Helen returned to her hair and resumed her singing, but her heart was no longer quite in it.

Gregory stepped out into the night air and scanned the darkness between the trees. The crack and spit of flame and the incessant din of the screech owls were the only sounds punctuating the quiet of the forest. It was unlike Lady Helen to be so easily spooked. And now her nerves seemed to have put him on edge too. Was he imagining it, or had he just heard footsteps? Out beyond the edge of the clearing?

Gregory looked to the other men, but they didn't appear to have heard anything. He moved forward, drawing his sword.

'Who's there?'

He peered into the night, blade at the ready. But, the only answer he received was from the owls hooting in the distance.

Back in the tent, Lady Helen was examining her reflection in her hand mirror. No doubt her maid would have declared her hair a job only half done, but she was reasonably satisfied with the results. In any case, she was keen to tuck herself into bed and forget her fears. A pleasant night's sleep, a little further to travel and she would be in Camelot by tomorrow evening. She laid the mirror down on the dressing table.

The tread of feet on foliage turned her head.

She put a hand to her chest, trying to still her galloping heart. Another silhouette loomed large on the tent wall. Again it swept like a dark ghost towards the entrance.

Lady Helen gasped. This shadow was that of a crooked and bent creature, entirely unfamiliar. This was not Gregory. She edged back on her stool, holding her breath. She opened her mouth, to call Gregory, but no sound came. As she struggled to find her voice, the shadow filled the tent flap.

Then the flap lifted and a face thrust its way inside. It was a horrible, drawn face, ashen and pale with deep-set, hard eyes that burned with hatred.

Despite the fear that threatened to freeze her where she sat, somehow Lady Helen found the strength to stand. She searched desperately and in vain for something she could say or do to banish this spectre.

The old woman stepped into the tent, her eyes burning, and let the flap fall closed behind her. She brought up her left hand – in it she clutched a crudely made straw doll – and began to mutter strange, harsh-sounding words. She was practically spitting them as she raised her right hand.

In it, a dagger flashed.

Lady Helen backed away. Again, she opened her mouth to cry out and there, at the back of her throat, she thought she might have found her voice at last.

But then the ancient woman brought the knife down, stabbing into the doll, cutting Lady Helen's voice dead. The old woman continued to mutter under her breath as she stabbed down again and again into the heart of the doll.

Lady Helen staggered backwards, staring at the blade shredding the straw and, feeling every wound. She was vaguely aware of her hand at her chest, searching for blood. But there was no wound. There was no mark.

Moments later Lady Helen slipped from consciousness and there was no more pain. No more light and no more shadows on the canvas. There was only the face of the old woman. And then only darkness.

Dead, Lady Helen fell back onto her bed. Her mouth hung open, vacant and graceless, her body an empty vessel that would make no more noise. Death put paid to beauty, but at least beauty could be borrowed.

That would be the next stage in the plan.

Mary Collins looked at the woman she had just slain. The lady was little more now than the straw doll she had used as a likeness. Her features were no doubt finer – pale cream skin and lustrous black hair – but ultimately she was made of materials that were just as perishable.

Mary sat her tired old body on the stool in front of the dressing table. Murmuring the necessary incantations, she clutched at the pendant that dangled from her neck. She felt its glow warming her gnarled fingers, felt the magic rising within her and infusing her with energies so alive they coursed through her veins like young blood, full of fire and vitality.

Something like warm air shifted and flowed over her. Her near-dead skin turned fluid as milk. Colours ran, rearranging themselves to fit the image she had in her mind. Then, she knew, it was done. Her new portrait was complete.

Her fingers reached up to feel the change. No wrinkles, no deep creases. And her hair, silken to the touch. She tugged a lock of it down in front of her eyes where she could admire its luxuriant darkness. Her hands too were smooth and soft.

She had to see.

Her gaze went to the hand mirror lying abandoned on the dressing table.

Tentatively she took a hold of it and lifted it in front of her face.

The truth stared back at her from the glass. Touching her cheek, she felt smooth and unblemished skin, but the reflection showed only her old face, like a mummified corpse. Time would not be denied completely. No matter. She did not need to fool mirrors. She needed only to fool the eyes of people: certain people in particular.

And as for time, she needed only enough to see Uther robbed of his one and only son.

*Arthur.*

# Chapter Four

Merlin blinked open his eyes to find his room flooded with sunlight. His room? His new room, his new *home*. And out there, all around, lay the grand city of Camelot. He could scarcely believe he had arrived. He yawned and stretched and sat up in bed, checking out his modest quarters.

With the addition of his clothes thrown on the floor, Merlin's new surroundings had begun to look a little more like home. His room contained a couple of wooden crates – one of which was now serving as a bedside table – a cupboard by the door, a bench under the window and a few stunted candles dotted about. Merlin thought Gaius had probably used the room as an extra place for storage, but now it was all his and Merlin couldn't help thinking that the old man had been exceptionally kind to hand over what little spare space he had, and at such short notice. Back home, nobody had had their own room; everybody shared one roof.

But all thoughts of his new room fled from Merlin's mind as he suddenly remembered the voice that had called to him in the night. It had called him by name, he was certain. *Merlin! Merlin!* . . . Surely it had to have been a dream? It was his first night in a new city, well, the first time he'd ever stayed in any city, so it wasn't surprising that his imagination was playing tricks on him.

He remembered the view outside his window. Now that – that was extraordinary. Well, he decided, there was no sense in lying around when there were so many things out there to do and see. Hauling himself out of bed, he started pulling on his clothes. He was starving too. He headed eagerly through into the next room, tugging on his jacket as he went.

His nose was pleasantly assaulted with an intriguing array of cooking smells and there was Gaius pottering at the stove. The old man acknowledged Merlin with a glance and gestured at a pail standing at one end of the table.

'I got you some water. You didn't have a wash last night.'

The old physician was right. How could he have forgotten!

Gaius looked up at Merlin and ladled some of whatever he was cooking into a bowl. Setting it down in front of the youngster, he invited Merlin to sit. 'Help yourself to breakfast.'

The magic words. Merlin squeezed past Gaius and gladly took the offered chair. Eagerly he examined the contents of the bowl.

He was looking at what he would have called gruel or slops or even possibly porridge. Except porridge sounded too fancy a word for what he saw in the bowl. Dipping in a spoon, he lifted a dollop of the mixture as close to his mouth as he dared then suddenly there was a thunk and a blur of movement and a shout from Gaius: 'Merlin!'

Merlin spun round to see the pail flying off the edge of the table. Golden fire flashed in his eyes and the bucket was suspended, just as Gaius had been, in mid-air. Time stopped. The spray of water, from the bucket, every pearly droplet, hung there too, like a frozen fountain.

Gaius stared at the pail. Then he turned his eyes on Merlin. The young warlock wondered if he'd done the right thing and instantly the bucket continued its fall, sloshing water all over the floorboards.

Gaius hopped backwards to avoid getting his feet wet, but continued to stare at Merlin. Now his expression was intense, demanding.

'How did you do that?'

So it had all been a test. Merlin knew he could be clumsy, but he was sure he hadn't so much as tapped the bucket with his elbow. He couldn't blame Gaius for his curiosity, but like the day before, Merlin was stuck for answers.

'Tell me,' insisted Gaius, his tone more fascinated than angry. 'I want to know. Did you incant a spell in your mind?'

Merlin looked up. 'I don't *know* any spells.'

'So what did you do?'

Merlin could only shrug. He wanted to get back to his breakfast. Even slops seemed appetizing all of a sudden.

'There must be something.'

Merlin's stomach rumbled. 'It just happens. I can't control it.'

Gaius continued to stare, mystified and perplexed. It was unnerving.

Merlin swallowed. If Gaius had meant to report him,

surely he would have done so last night. And he wouldn't have gone to the trouble of finding out more this morning, would he? Although Merlin trusted his mother's instincts, sending him to Gaius, he still wished he could be totally sure. 'What are you going to do?'

Gaius blinked, for a moment apparently unsure what he was talking about. Then he twigged. 'It's not me you need to worry about.' He let out a weary sigh. 'You can help me out until I find you some paid work.'

Merlin felt a wave of relief. The old man had shown him only kindness and he shouldn't have doubted him. He smiled at Gaius, pleased to have found a friend he could trust with his secret – and so soon after his arrival. His mother had been right to send him to this man.

Gaius wandered off to a nearby bench and collected a couple of phials, each containing a small measure of brightly coloured liquid. 'Here.' He presented them to Merlin, one at a time. Merlin wondered what they might be. 'Hollyhock and feverfew for Lady Percival. And this is for Sir Owain. He's as blind as a weevil. Tell him not to take all of it at once.'

Pleased that Gaius had decided he could stay, Merlin pocketed both the phials. A few light duties were the least he could do to repay the physician's hospitality and his trust.

As Merlin headed for the door, Gaius handed him a bacon sandwich. 'Here.' There was almost a paternal quality about the old man's smile. And a sly twinkle in his eye that suggested he had been planning to give Merlin the sandwich all along. 'Off you go.'

Merlin took the sandwich gratefully. Happy to be armed with something tasty to eat, he grinned and reached for the door handle. This round of deliveries might also afford him a chance to explore the city some more and Merlin couldn't wait.

Gaius called after him, the old man's voice striking a concerned note this time. 'And Merlin . . .'

Merlin stopped and looked back at Gaius.

'I don't need to tell you, but the practise of any form of enchantments will get you killed. D'you understand that?'

Merlin nodded and set out on his errands.

# Chapter Five

All Merlin saw of Lady Percival was the narrow strip of face she deigned to show through the crack in the door.

'Well, where's Gaius? What have you done with Gaius?' she asked nervously.

'He's . . . busy, that's all. He asked me to deliver this.' Merlin held out the tiny bottle. 'I'm his new assistant.'

There was a long pause in which Merlin felt himself the subject of intense scrutiny. 'Very well then, give it to me.'

Merlin sighed, relieved, and handed over the phial. A hand darted out and snatched it. 'I shan't take it though,' she said.

'What? No, but you have to. It's—' medicine, he was going to say.

'It could be anything,' she declared. 'No, I shall take it back to Gaius. I'm not drinking anything until he's had a look at it.'

'No, don't do that—'

The door shut in his face. Oh dear, Merlin could see it now: his first delivery and Lady Feverfew – as he decided to call her from that moment on – turns up later at Gaius' chambers, querying the very medicine he's made for her.

Merlin gazed at the door for a moment, wondering if there was anything else he could do. Deciding the answer was probably not he shrugged and headed off on his next delivery.

Sir Owain was easy enough to find after a few enquiries and soon Merlin was knocking at another door. The man who answered didn't look much like a 'sir', but he guessed not many men did when they were relaxing at home. Merlin was just glad the man had thrown the door open wide rather than hidden behind it as Lady Feverfew had done.

Sir Owain squinted at his visitor and seemed about to ask him many of the same questions as Lady Feverfew: who was he and what had he done with Gaius?

'I've brought you your medicine,' said Merlin, proffering the phial quickly.

Owain blinked, then nodded. He reached out for the bottle, but his hand was aiming too low and too far to the left. Merlin plonked the phial in his palm. Gratefully the fellow popped the tiny cork and raised the bottle to his lips . . .

'Gaius said not to take it all at once . . .' But already, before Merlin had finished speaking, the man had gulped it down in one. Merlin managed a feeble smile. 'I'm sure it's fine.'

His chores done, Merlin strolled back in the general direction of Gaius' chambers. The sun was shining and he decided it might be the perfect time to take in some of the city's sights. He was in no hurry, it was a fine day and there was much more of Camelot to see.

He wandered through a gate and into the training yard. An impressive range of weapons was on display, on tables and in racks arranged around the yard. The cobbles were littered with straw from the practice dummies and a number of large round wooden shields for archery targets.

At the moment, there were no hard-working knights to be seen. A group of lads around Merlin's age was gathered near the targets.

Merlin would have liked to see them practising, but there didn't seem to be much going on right now – maybe they were taking a break. Merlin started to walk on, eager to see as much of the city as possible, when he heard someone call out, 'Morris!'

Glancing over in the direction of the shout, he saw a straggly-haired and shabbily dressed young manservant come hurrying in answer to the call. A lad dressed in a smart red tunic and a few pieces of armour was now standing a little apart from the rest of the group. He was fair-haired, solidly built and had a slightly haughty look about him.

'Where is the target?' he demanded of the manservant.

Morris looked so keen to please this lad, Merlin recognized something of himself in him. 'Over there, sir.' Morris pointed to a wooden shield that had been mounted on stumpy wooden legs to serve as a target.

The young master arched a brow and pointed skyward. 'It's into the sun.'

The servant searched the broad expanse of blue. 'Well, it's not that bright, sir.'

'Bit like you then.'

The group laughed and Merlin chuckled quietly to himself. The poor servant had walked right into that one.

Villages or cities, some things never changed. There were always gangs and it was always easy to spot the leaders. Back home, Merlin had been teased as much as the next boy, but as he'd grown up he'd found ways to repay it – usually later, with a subtle trick or two of his own – without his tormentors ever knowing it was him.

Poor Morris didn't have that option. Instead he defended his original placement of the shield. 'Well, you've got to be able to fight in all weathers, sir.'

The leader of the pack found that intensely amusing. 'And what would you know about fighting?'

Morris had no answer to that and bowed to the inevitable. 'I'll put the target down the other end, shall I, sir?'

Taking his master's nod as his cue, he ran to the target and picked it up. It was large and unwieldy and he was hidden behind it, looking like a big disc of wood on legs as he carried it off towards the opposite end of the yard.

The group's ringleader turned to one of his lackeys and said, laughing, 'This'll teach him.'

To Merlin's surprise, the lad drew a dagger and hurled it at the target.

It thunked into the wood, dead centre.

Morris popped his head up from behind the shield – staring boggle-eyed at the dagger sticking out from the bull's eye.

'Hey! Hang on!'

The gang burst out laughing. Even Merlin had to admit it was a comical sight, although the flinging of knives was a tad too dangerous for his comedy tastes.

The ringleader gestured for Morris to keep moving. 'Don't stop.'

The servant nodded, his head ducking back out of sight as he bore the shield further along and placed the target down. 'Here?'

'I told you to keep moving,' shouted the lad in red.

Morris looked out from behind the shield again, set to ask a question . . .

. . . then was obliged to duck as a second dagger came flying his way. The blade bit deep into the wood. Morris flinched as though it had struck him in the belly.

The group of friends seemed to be really enjoying the terrified expression on the servant's face. But

Merlin had stopped chuckling. This was getting beyond a joke and had strayed into outright bullying. And Merlin knew what that felt like. Glancing upwards he noticed a maid leaning out of a window, a look of disapproval on her face as she beat a rug against the sill.

The ringleader was keen to keep the joke going. 'Come on, we want some moving target practice!'

Swallowing, Morris hefted up the target again and picked his way nervously along the yard. Suddenly he took cover as another dagger thudded into the shield. This guy in the red tunic was really good with his knife-throwing – but that wouldn't be making the experience any more pleasant for Morris.

'Run!' his young master urged him.

Morris needed no further encouragement. He quickened his pace, although there was no actual escape. So of course he ended up darting this way and that – just a shield and a pair of boots, a slew of daggers chasing him, thunk-thunking into their target and encouraging him to run even faster.

Until finally he stumbled on the cobbles and went flying. The wooden target went cartwheeling away. Merlin saw it trundling towards him and he was preparing to hop out of its path, but gradually it lost its momentum and wobbled to a stop at his feet.

The gang were in fits of laughter all over again.

'Come on, pick it up again.' The ringleader smiled at his gaggle of followers and they started collecting more daggers from a nearby bench where a host of weapons were laid out. The lads handed them to a lieutenant, who was all set to pass them onto their leader as required. They were all ready for another round.

Morris dragged himself up off the ground and came trotting obediently over, stooping to retrieve the shield. Merlin had had enough. He planted his foot on the wood, pinning it in place on the cobbles. These guys were through using Morris for their target practice.

'Hurry up!' the chief bully called over.

Morris looked up at Merlin with an appeal, clearly not wanting any trouble.

Merlin gave him a reassuring smile, then called across to the ringleader. 'Hey, come on, that's enough.' Best keep it as friendly as possible, he decided.

The leader didn't seem like he'd got the message – at least, not the friendly part.

'What?'

Breaking off from the pack, he swaggered over, a

cocky and amused look aimed squarely at Merlin. Apparently he wasn't too bothered about having his sport interrupted. And why would he be – when there was more fun to be had?

Suddenly the gang and their leader had a new target.

# Chapter Six

Morris hooked his fingers under the shield and tried to lift it as a means of encouraging Merlin to take his foot off the target. 'It's all right,' he assured Merlin. As fearful as he had been of the flying daggers, he was plainly more anxious about whatever punishments his master might dish out.

The thought of this only made Merlin more determined to see it through. The young man walking towards him wasn't *his* master and he refused to be intimidated by his broad shoulders or his air of self-importance.

He kept his foot firmly on the shield. 'No, it's not,' he said firmly.

The pack leader came to a halt in front of Merlin. He didn't seem happy with his decision.

'You've had your fun, my friend,' Merlin added.

As annoyed as the young man had seemed seconds earlier, he seemed even more angry to be ordered about. He frowned. 'Do I know you?'

'I'm Merlin.'

'So I don't know you.'

'No.' Even Merlin had to admit that the introductions could have gone better.

'But you called me "friend".'

There was an awkward silence. Merlin glanced about to see they had drawn an audience: both his opponent's gang and a few passers-by who sensed something brewing.

Merlin pressed on, knowing he was sticking up for someone and was right to do so, 'That was my mistake.'

The lad nodded. 'I think so.'

'Yeah. I'd never have a friend who could be such an ass.' Merlin laughed and glanced at the small crowd of spectators. A few of them joined in – hopefully that might help persuade the leader to stop being such an idiot.

'Or I, one who could be so stupid,' replied the lad in red.

Merlin was about to scoff. It wasn't a particularly good retort. But before Merlin could say anything,

the local lad had laid his hand on the hilt of his sword
– prompting the audience to take a step back.

If his smile was anything to go by, the lad enjoyed
throwing his weight around and enjoyed it even
more when people reacted to the threat of his sword.
Merlin decided he had made his point and turned
to leave.

Apparently the ringleader wasn't finished with him
though. 'Tell me, Merlin, d'you know how to walk on
your knees?'

The gang of lads brayed like donkeys. They were still
enjoying the show. Merlin turned back to face his
would-be tormentor. 'No,' he said, more calmly than
he felt.

'Well, I suggest you learn,' came the lad's reply.

Merlin decided the best way to deal with this
worsening situation was to grin and laugh it all off. It
was probably all bluff anyway. There was no way he was
kneeling for this prat.

The lad on the other hand seemed surprised that
Merlin wasn't kneeling already. 'D'you want me to
help you?'

He'd tried to be calm, but Merlin felt his fists tighten,
anger rising inside him. This lad was taking things too
far. He'd had no right to treat Morris in such an awful

way and now he had no right to mock Merlin in front of his mates.

'I wouldn't if I were you,' warned Merlin.

'Why, what are you going to do to me?'

'You've no idea . . . '

'Be my guest.' The young man drew nearer and seemed to stand taller. Evidently he was about as intimidated by threats as Merlin had been by the hand on the sword hilt. His shoulders looked even broader this close. Despite himself, Merlin stepped back a pace.

Which of course was what the bully had been looking for.

'Come on, then . . . ' He beckoned, egging Merlin on.

Merlin felt his face go hot – only a blush, thank goodness. He mustn't use magic here of all places. That'd be the quickest way to win the fight – but he'd almost certainly lose his life into the bargain. He'd warned the lad, and now he had to back up his boast with something. He was aware – again – of his fists clenched at his side, and throwing a punch was all he could think to do.

He aimed for the lad's jaw, there was a blur of motion and suddenly his foe had Merlin's arm in his grip. Then he jerked Merlin swiftly round and yanked his arm up behind his back. Hard. Merlin grimaced. Ouch.

His voice was close in Merlin's ear. 'I'll have you thrown in jail for that.'

Now Merlin did scoff, through the pain. 'Who d'you think you are – the king!'

After a short pause, the lad replied, 'No, I'm his son – Arthur.'

*Prince Arthur.* Ouch, again.

Merlin realized with a horrible sinking feeling; he was in deep trouble now.

'On your knees,' Arthur barked.

Merlin felt a kick to the back of his legs and he folded into a kneeling position. He opened his mouth to object and was all ready to fight his way to a stand when he saw the guards closing in on him.

Merlin's protests fell on deaf ears as he was marched away from the square. Once inside the palace, he was led down the dungeon stairs and then pushed into the nearest vacant cell. An uneven mound of straw and sacking broke his fall. He turned his head in time to see the cell door clang shut.

Merlin stayed where he was for a moment, exhausted.

Getting thrown in a dungeon on your first day in a new city, now that was quite an achievement . . .

Moments later, having moved into a more comfortable position, he surveyed his surroundings. Modest though the garret room that Gaius had given him was, Merlin much preferred it to his new quarters.

Thinking of Gaius and how kind the old physician had already been, Merlin felt mortified, picturing Gaius' reaction when word reached him of his new apprentice's imprisonment. Merlin knew he couldn't have just walked by and let Arthur treat his servant the way he had, but he wished it had turned out better than this.

He couldn't do anything about the past now. But alone in jail he began to wonder: just how serious an offence had he committed? His punch hadn't landed, but technically he had assaulted the king's son. He knew he was in a lot of trouble, but what if it was even worse than he'd feared?

Surely they wouldn't leave him here to rot? (Although it smelled like they'd left a few others to rot.) He'd only acted as he'd thought just and right.

# Chapter Seven

Mary Collins stared across the valley at the white walls of the city of Camelot. The city where her son was buried. No, not even that. As a practitioner of magic, a condemned man, he would not be granted burial within the city cemetery, but instead his remains would be disposed of in some lonely plot far beyond the walls.

'It's late, my lady,' said Gregory as he brought his horse alongside that of the woman he thought was Lady Helen.

She had no idea how long they had paused here on the crest of this hill, looking at their destination. She glanced at Gregory and managed to force a smile. He had reminded her of more than just the hour. He had reminded her that she was not Mary Collins. Not any more.

It had been a hard day. They were all anxious for the journey to be over. She gave him a nod and spurred her horse on, down the track to meet the road to Camelot. She was keen to be inside those walls. Then her real work could begin.

The night before, Mary Collins had slept in the same tent as the dead Lady Helen. She'd left Lady Helen's body sprawled where she had dropped, on the bed, and had herself slept on the floor. Only then, before sleep, had she thought of her son, lying cold and alone.

In the morning, she'd expected her old bones to ache and creak from such an unforgiving bed. But she felt no physical pain, just an ache in her heart, and *that* ache would never go away. Her transformation was more than just an illusion – her bones, her muscle and sinew were all young again. Mary Collins smiled to herself; her disguise was even more convincing than she'd dared hope.

From now on, she had told herself, you are no longer just Mary Collins. You are Lady Helen. You sing like an angel, but you harbour the heart of a murderess.

She hadn't left the tent straight away, but instead had waited for daylight. As the sun rose, she began to chant

52

over the body of Lady Helen, calling forth a fire to burn each particle of flesh and bone. Heat and light had flared up, turning the body to ash, ash that had transformed into tiny pinpricks of light before dwindling away to nothing. Such a display would surely have given her away by casting great shadows on the tent walls had she performed the deed at night. She was confident that she could have overpowered the guards, but it would have looked very strange for Lady Helen to arrive in Camelot without her escort.

When she emerged from the tent she tried to apologize for her tardiness, but Gregory assured her that they could easily make up the time and that he still hoped to reach the citadel by nightfall.

'Lady Helen' had approved of the plan.

The weather soon closed in and the ride became increasingly difficult – wind and rain blew hard into their faces, lashing their horses and muddying the tracks. But she had ridden on, unabated. Mary Collins had not felt so alive in a long time. The storm merely seemed to echo her mood: dark and full of intent.

'Lady Helen' was at the head of her small escort as they rode in through the gates of Camelot. The guards waved them on into the courtyard. 'Lady Helen' was so pleased to find herself in the heart of her enemy's citadel that her horse had barely halted before she dismounted. She looked up the steps, to the great doors of the palace.

Suddenly out of the corner of her eye, 'Lady Helen' thought she'd glimpsed something moving. She glanced down at her feet. From a puddle of rainwater, Mary Collins stared back at her. Clearly nature could still see through her disguise.

She hurried on up the steps, before any of the guards thought to gaze down at the puddles. It had been a long journey and she was eager to get into the warm – perfect pretexts for haste.

Morgana had done all she could to state her case and now she was doing what she was told. It was late and the throne room was rather gloomy, but the gathered courtiers, all dressed in their finery, added plenty of splashes of colour.

Morgana, for her part, had also made an effort and dressed up. Whatever her quarrels with Uther, she had decided it simply wasn't fair to take that out on Lady Helen.

Her maid, Gwen, was at her side for company, although they couldn't enjoy any of their usual gossip. With everyone else waiting quietly on their guest's arrival, even whispered conversations would have carried a shade too loudly.

Arthur, meanwhile, had stopped by long enough to make his excuses to his father, then swaggered past and favoured her with a smug wink on the way out. Typical. She had to be present by royal command, while the prince could absent himself, claiming guard duty or whatever. Just like Arthur to cite one set of responsibilities to shirk another, she thought with a smile. Privately she had to admire his ingenuity though. Not that she'd ever tell him that.

If only she'd had guard duties, she might have done the same. Oh well, it was too late now.

Resplendent in a gown of very royal purple, Lady Helen swept in through the open doorway and up the length of the hall. Morgana remembered the lady's last visit and it struck her that there was a greater confidence to her stride, possibly born of familiarity, as though she felt more at home here with each visit. The king rose to greet her. Of course, Uther always made her feel as comfortable in Camelot as he possibly could.

'Lady Helen.' The formality of his greeting was transparent. Morgana smiled at the telltale tremor of affection that softened Uther's characteristic steel. 'Thank you so much for coming to sing at our celebrations.'

'The pleasure is all mine,' Lady Helen murmured.

Lady Helen was certainly beautiful. Her skin was pale and her dark hair framed a smooth, round face. Uther took her proffered hand and raised it to his lips, for all the world looking like a lovestruck boy. 'How was your journey?' he enquired.

'Oh,' she sighed. 'The time it took, sire.'

'I know, but it's always worth the wait,' Uther continued.

'It will be,' Lady Helen said simply. She reached up to toy with the pendant at her neck. It looked to be a beautiful gemstone in quite a simple setting. Then she glanced at the king and smiled. She was sure the end result would be worth her long journey.


On his first night Merlin had been so excited to be looking out over the rooftops of Camelot. On this, his second night, there was nothing to look at apart from the walls, the bars and the straw covering the floor of his cell.

He guessed the idea was for the prisoner to reflect on his crimes. He'd done his fair share of that – and spent the rest of the time blaming Arthur. After all, Arthur had been the one picking on his servant and when Merlin had been ready to let the matter drop, Arthur had been the one to press the point. Merlin soon grew tired of going over the day's events and tried to focus instead on thinking of ways he could escape or persuade the guards that the situation had been completely blown out of all proportion and that they should release him.

Sleep eventually came, but tonight someone – or something – wouldn't allow him any rest.

*Merlin!*

The voice seemed to call him from outside his dreams as though trying to wake him from his sleep.

*Merlin!*

Somewhere in the depths. A voice bellowed to him from below.

*Merlin!*

The voice pulled at him and suddenly he felt like he was falling.

*Merlin!*

Then, in his mind, he thought he saw something – a glow, like a golden ghost. It danced and flickered like a flame.

*Merlin!*

The sound seemed to be coming from the glow – Merlin tried to make out a discernible shape, but couldn't quite see one. All he knew was that the light must be coming from something powerful, something magical – he could feel it.

And by now it was bellowing his name.

*MERLIN!*

# Chapter Eight

Sunlight streamed in through the bars of the cell window. Merlin snapped awake and rolled over on the straw, the voice he'd heard in his dreams reverberating in his head like an echo. It seemed too real somehow, as though he had brought it with him from the realm of sleep and into the harsh reality of his cell.

He frowned. Had he just heard it again? He pressed his ear to the ground, listening for any sound.

'Merlin!'

He gave a start. But this time the voice sounded very different. It was too loud, too familiar – and came from behind him. Merlin spun round to see Gaius being admitted by a guard. The physician didn't look too happy. 'You never cease to *amaze* me!'

Merlin jumped to his feet, but resisted the temptation to smile. As pleased as he was to see the old man, Gaius didn't seem to be in the mood for greetings.

'The one thing someone like you should do is keep your head down, and what do you do?'

Merlin felt bad; he'd been here a day and the one friend he had made in Camelot so far he'd managed to let down. 'I'm sorry.'

Gaius' tone softened, but still carried a slight warning note. 'You're lucky. I've pulled a few strings to get you released.'

Merlin couldn't believe his luck. Gaius really was a good friend. 'Oh, thank you, thank you. I won't forget this.'

'Ah, well . . . ' Gaius waved him down before he got too carried away. 'There *is* a small price to pay.'

Merlin felt slightly nervous at this piece of news, but, well, how bad could it be? He was getting out of here, that was the main thing.

Thoroughly rotten was the answer, as it turned out. The tomatoes thrown at him were really mushy – as he looked up one splattered across the left side of his face. As for the smell – there had been smells like it in his cell, but he'd never expected to encounter them again in a piece of fruit. He was sure he could feel a trickle of juice on his forehead, threatening to dribble seeds down into his eye.

Well, he wouldn't be able to do anything about it if it did – he was securely locked in the stocks. He would just have to put up with whatever the small band of children that had gathered found to throw at him.

The tomato was swiftly followed by a barrage of stinking cabbage, clumps of damp potato peel and other vegetable matter less easily identified. Nearby, Gaius chortled as the assortment of leftovers and unwanted scraps pelted Merlin in the face.

'Thanks,' Merlin told him, blinking as he felt the tomato seeds run down towards his eye at last.

Gaius wandered away, still chuckling to himself and leaving Merlin to take his punishment on the chin and anywhere else the small army of children cared to aim.

Then, unexpectedly, after another volley of mulchy missiles, the attacks eased off. Merlin squinted to see the children running away, their baskets empty but their hearts full of cheer.

Oh well, at least he had paid his price, thought Merlin. Hopefully a guard would be along soon to let him out of this contraption.

In fact, he sensed the shadow of someone drawing

near right then. He craned his neck for a proper look: even if it was a grizzled-faced guard it would be a happy sight if he had come to set him free. But the sight of a girl was something far better.

Pretty, dark-skinned, her hair arranged in an attractive nest of ringlets, she just stood there for a moment, looking at him with her big bright eyes and gentle smile.

Merlin returned the smile through a screen of pulp and tomato seeds.

'I'm Guinevere,' she said. 'But most people call me Gwen,' she continued. 'I'm the Lady Morgana's maid.'

'Right. I'm Merlin.' He waggled a hand. Graciously Gwen accepted what was the best effort at a handshake Merlin could manage right at that moment. 'Although most people call me "idiot".'

She shook her head. 'No, I saw what you did. It was so brave.'

Merlin couldn't quite place her, but, it was really nice of her to come and speak to him.

'It was stupid,' said Merlin.

'Well, I'm glad you turned away. You weren't going to beat him.'

He laughed. 'Oh, I could beat him.'

Gwen appeared to size him up all over again. 'Yeah? You think? Because you don't look like one of those big muscly fellows . . .'

'Thanks,' replied Merlin.

'No,' she protested. 'I'm sure you're stronger than you look . . . It's just – Arthur's one of those real rough, tough, save-the-world kind of men and, well . . .'

'What?' Merlin encouraged her to finish the sentence.

'You don't look like that.'

So there was the hard truth: he, Merlin, didn't look like a rough, tough, save-the-world type. Luckily she wasn't telling him anything he didn't know, so he could take it. He invited her a little closer with a conspiratorial tilt of his head. 'I'm in disguise.'

Gwen grinned. She refrained from drawing any closer though, put off by his vegetable-based perfume. 'Well,' she commended, 'it was great you stood up to him.'

Merlin was afraid she was getting ready to depart. He didn't doubt she had things to do, places to be, but he was enjoying the conversation too much to let her go just now.

'You think so?'

'Arthur's a bully.' That much Merlin had figured

out for himself. 'And everyone thought you were a real hero.'

'Oh, yeah?' He recalled the members of the crowd who'd laughed at the line he'd given Arthur. It probably took courage to laugh at the crown prince's expense. It had never occurred to him that they might actually admire him for making a stand. Musing, he looked past Gwen and the sight that greeted him cut his thoughts short.

Oh well, time really did fly when you were having fun, and all good things really did come to an end. There was no sense in arguing with fate. 'Excuse me,' he said, gently motioning Gwen aside with a rather limited wave of his hand.

She followed his glance and saw the band of children, their baskets full to the brim with fresh ammunition.

'My fans are waiting.'

Gwen needed no further prompting. She ducked out of the line of fire and, with an apologetic but kindly wave goodbye, hastened off on her errands.

Amid roars and cheers, the children opened fire.

# Chapter Nine

Thankfully the children ran out of vegetable scraps again before too long and Merlin was left on his own for a while. Eventually a pair of guards wandered over to release him with a warning. Merlin promised them he wouldn't do it again and, pausing only to rub his wrists, he raced off back to Gaius' chambers.

The old physician had thoughtfully fetched him a bowl of clean water and left it out on a bench. Merlin felt so much better having washed his face clean of vegetable remains.

Gaius was hovering at the table, having dished up some chicken broth and a hunk of bread. Merlin sat himself down without a word and drank in the aromas of cooked meat and freshly baked bread. It reminded him what the word 'fresh' meant.

Setting the pot back on the stove, Gaius gestured

at the plate. 'D'you want some vegetables with that?'

Merlin met the old man's smile with one of his own. He toyed at his food with his fork, knowing he still had some apologizing to do. 'I know you're still angry with me.'

Gaius sat down opposite Merlin, hunched over the table. He regarded the young warlock earnestly. 'Your mother asked me to look after you.'

'Yes.' Merlin was beginning to appreciate what a big responsibility that was for someone to take on — especially someone he hadn't even known before yesterday. His mother had never really told him much about how she knew Gaius, but she had been sure he would take good care of him.

'What d'you think *she* would say?'

Merlin started forking up a few mouthfuls of food — if only to avoid the topic for a short while. It wasn't easy with Gaius watching him.

The old man broke the silence. 'What did she say to you about your gifts?'

Merlin shrugged. 'That I was special.'

Gaius nodded. 'You *are* special. The likes of which I've never seen before.'

Merlin studied the old man's face. He had lived a long time; he must have seen something of magic, before it had become outlawed by royal decree. He had supposed magic had been commonplace back then, but perhaps not. Either way, here was Gaius, who must have seen it all, telling him – Merlin – that he had never seen the likes of his gift before. That sounded like a weighty revelation – or would have done, if Merlin could figure out what it might mean.

'Why?' he said. He badly wanted to know what made him different, wanted to know what it had been like before, when practising magic hadn't been a crime.

'Magic requires incantations, spells. It takes years of study.' Gaius looked for the right words, thinking back to the incident with the pail and his fall from the balcony. 'What I saw you do – it was – *elemental*. Instinctive.'

Merlin didn't know if those were the right words. He hadn't given it that level of thought before now, no more than a bird gave thought to the power of flight – it simply spread its wings and flew. Back at home he had at least had some fun with his powers, although he had known they weren't something he could reveal to just anyone. But here he was expected to keep them totally hidden.

'What's the point if it can't be used?'

Gaius shrugged sympathetically. 'That I don't know.

You are a question that has never been posed before, Merlin.'

Merlin glanced at the books filling the shelves behind Gaius. Surely in all that great store of knowledge there were answers. But if what Gaius was saying were true, well, if a question hadn't been asked before, nobody would have come up with an answer.

'Did you ever study magic?'

There was, Merlin sensed, a veritable treasure trove of secrets locked up in the pause that followed his question.

'Uther banned all such work twenty years ago,' Gaius said eventually.

Merlin knew that much already. But why did Uther have to go and ban *all* magic? There were plenty of good uses, plenty of good things that could be done with such a gift. Plenty that *he* could do. 'But why?'

Gaius hesitated again, but this time only to shape his explanation. 'Magic corrupts, Merlin. You're too young to know – people used magic for the wrong ends back then. It threw the natural order into chaos. Uther made it his mission to destroy everything from that time. Even the Dragons.'

Merlin sat up. He hadn't expected that – Dragons.

Beasts from fairy tales with scales and wings and fiery breath, Dragons were monstrous in size and yet nowhere to be seen except in stories. He vaguely recalled his mother speaking to him at bedtime of how such creatures had once been real, and it had been fun to imagine them soaring across the skies, lurking in caves and sitting on mountains of gold. But Merlin had never been sure whether he believed his mother's tales or not.

Now here was someone as wise as Gaius, speaking of them as though they were real. Not only that, but a king had taken them seriously enough to set out to destroy them.

'Why?'

'He feared them,' said Gaius gravely. 'So he had them slaughtered.'

Merlin blinked. That didn't make any sense. To wipe out an entire species because of fear was dreadful, incomprehensible. Merlin thought of all the tales about Dragons he had heard, the pictures of them he had envisaged in his imagination. And it occurred to him now that he would never see one. Surely some must have escaped the terrible slaughter. 'What – all of them?'

Gaius cleared his throat as though not quite sure how to continue. 'There was one Dragon he chose not to kill, but to keep as an example. He imprisoned it in a cave deep beneath the castle. Where no one can free it.'

Merlin stared, feeling his eyes grow wider. Unbidden, he was thinking of the voice: the voice that had called to him, up through the stones to reach into his dreams, into his very soul. Only the word 'Dragon' seemed sufficient to match the power of that lone voice. And here Gaius was telling him of a single magical beast, the last of his kind, and it was imprisoned where? Underneath the castle.

It couldn't be. It was just too fantastic. Why would a Dragon be calling to him? No, it was just his imagination running wild, excited by all these revelations. He wondered if he should tell Gaius of his dream. But Gaius already had other things on his mind.

'Now, eat up. I've got some more errands for you to run,' Gaius said, breaking into the young warlock's thoughts. The old man stood and, collecting a handful of items from the nearby bench, pushed a short succession of phials and pouches across the table to Merlin, closing the subject of magic and Dragons, locking them away, Merlin hoped for another day.

Merlin looked down at the handful of remedies, nodding as he registered his instructions and noting each of the remedies as Gaius explained them. Happy to repay some of the kindness the old physician had shown him, Merlin headed off to make these new deliveries.

# Chapter Ten

Wormwood for Master Henry's lice. Buckbean for Sir Casper's case of worms. The list of deliveries this time round was a colourful one. In some cases, Merlin had trouble deciding which sounded worse, the ailment or the remedy. But as he delivered each item he was pleased to note that today's house calls were going smoothly and without incident.

Some of the people on his rounds were very friendly – even inviting him in – but after Master Henry, Merlin politely declined, just handing over the medicines at arm's length. Of course, he also had some fun making up names, so added Sir Casper Buckbean and Master Henry Wormwood to his list.

After a few other stops, he set off on the final delivery. He had saved the best till last.

Lady Helen.

The phial in his hand supposedly contained some lotion or potion for her voice. So Gaius had said. Idly Merlin wondered whether it would make him able to sing like a nightingale if he took a swig. Hmm, he thought, it was doubtful.

As usual he had to ask for directions, but he soon found himself jogging up some steps to a brightly lit gallery landing lined with pillars and stained-glass windows. At the far end, he found the door to Lady Helen's chamber. He lifted a hand to knock, wondering what kind of woman she might be.

He gathered she was some special guest of the king. And when he had asked the way to her chambers, people had been in awe: starstruck and envious. One old fellow had practically begged for the chance to make the delivery in his stead. Merlin had laughed and apologized, telling the old boy that he was sorry but that he was expected to deliver the phial in person. If anything, the encounter had left him keener than ever to meet this lady.

Merlin paused outside her door, feeling slightly intimidated. You're simply here to hand over her medicine, he told himself, just get on with it, report to Gaius, job well done – and maybe he'll let you off for the afternoon. See some more of the city and stay out of trouble.

It sounded like a great plan for the day.

Merlin rapped his knuckles on the door.

There was no answer – but the door creaked open.

Maybe he could just take the phial in and leave? Spurred on by the fact that things had gone smoothly so far today, he nudged the door open a little further and peered inside.

Sumptuous was the first word that struck him to describe the room – it was the sort of room he might have expected to find reserved for a princess. Lady Helen was obviously well looked after here.

There were velvet-cushioned chairs and gold drapes everywhere, with a hearty blaze going in the fireplace. A vase of delicate purple flowers added a further splash of colour.

Atop the dressing table stood a large mirror – only to be expected in a lady's room, Merlin thought – but someone had carelessly thrown a shawl over it. It seemed a bit untidy compared to the rest of the room, but Merlin wasn't about to judge; he was conscious that the state of his own room left a little to be desired. Thankfully Gaius hadn't ventured in there since he'd taken up residence.

Picking his way across the room carefully, Merlin reached the dressing table and set the phial down among the hairbrushes, perfumes, powders and other cosmetics that were strewn across the top. There was even a fancy gold goblet. As Merlin gazed at the clutter, he suddenly noticed a very strange object – a straw doll. Merlin frowned. He didn't know much of ladies' accessories, but this one struck him as a bit out of place.

He picked it up and turned it over in his hand. A childhood toy? Sentimental value? He didn't think so, unless the Lady Helen had been very poor as a child. Even in his home village, the woodcarver could generally knock you up a wooden doll. Besides, there seemed to be a slightly sinister quality to the thing. The straw was rough and coarse and the doll even appeared to be damaged, with gouges in the middle where its chest was. Whether it was these wounds or something else, something about the doll made him nervous. He set it down again, as close to the exact same angle and position as he could manage – as far as he could estimate.

Something else caught his eye then – something with a jewellery box sitting on top of it and half covered by a decorative cloth. Merlin couldn't resist. He shifted the jewellery box and flicked aside the cloth . . .

Mary Collins strode along the gallery landing in mixed spirits. Her reception with the king had gone well, but there had been no sign of Arthur.

Her disguise had passed the test of Uther's inspection. The king's ward, Morgana, had greeted her with accomplished courtesy and politeness and Mary had detected no suspicion from either of them about her identity. Afterwards she had checked in with Gregory – because that was what the real Lady Helen would have been expected to do – to ensure that he and his men were taken care of, garrisoned with the loyal soldiers of Camelot.

Her duties for now were fulfilled. She had earned some respite. She paused, her senses twitching. Straight ahead, she saw immediately that something was amiss.

The door to her chambers was open. She quickened her pace. If she had been discovered, there might still be time to nip that discovery in the bud.


Under the cloth, Merlin had unveiled a book.

Its leather binding was encrusted with age and embossed with gold leaf. It was fastened closed with a length of old string and an ornate clasp. If the doll didn't belong, then the same was true of this – even more so. Except somehow the two objects seemed to belong together. If he opened it, would he find some reference to the doll, he wondered . . .

Tentatively he tested the string.

But then he heard the tap of footsteps on stone somewhere down the passage.

He turned to glance at the doorway. There was no sign of anybody – yet. But someone was definitely coming.

Seized by panic and guilt, he hastened to replace the book, lay the cloth over it and set the jewellery box on top. His hands moved in such a flurry that he managed to catch the shawl that was draped over the mirror and it dropped onto the dressing table knocking the goblet over with a clatter. Merlin winced and reached to set the goblet upright.

He heard the slow tap of shoes on the floor behind him. He felt the rapid pounding of his own heart. He turned.

There was a woman standing just inside the doorway.

She stared at him with cold suspicion. He smiled, but that didn't seem to help.

'What are you doing here?' she demanded sternly.

He could see his future – his very near future – and in it she was calling the guards. Whatever she needed the preparation for, he felt sure that her voice would be in fine enough form for that.

Her eyes darted past him, as though searching for

signs of disturbance. Whatever she saw, there was a pale cloud – something like fear – that passed over her features. For some reason, it silenced her and she didn't call the guards. Only waited.

'I was asked to deliver this.'

Quickly Merlin reached behind him and scooped up the phial from the dressing table. He dashed over and gave it to her.

She took it, a look on her face that suggested she didn't care for servants in such close quarters. Then she motioned with her head and stood aside. The signal was clear: get out.

Merlin wasted no time. He skirted round her and beat a hasty retreat out the door. All the while, he was anxious about whether she would report the intrusion. But there was something more that preyed on his mind. Something about the doll, something about the book. More especially, something about the way she had looked when she'd glanced past him. What could she have seen that had scared her?

Nothing, Merlin was sure, that could have frightened her as much as she had scared him.

Mary Collins continued to stare at the image of her true face in the mirror.

Whatever the boy had been doing, he had disturbed her carefully arranged shawl. Probably no more than a meddling, over-curious servant. But she could ill afford to be found out by anyone, no matter how low their calling. Fortunately for him he had not turned round and seen her real face.

Oh, if he had turned and caught so much as a glimpse of her reflection, he would have been dealt the fright of his life. And then—

Then she would have had to kill him.

# Chapter Eleven

Out in the passage, Merlin paused in the light of one of the stained-glass windows. Looking back he saw the door slam shut. He should be glad, he supposed, that it had slammed with him on the *out*side. He hurried on his way before she had a chance to change her mind and call the guards.

He felt a bit guilty. He shouldn't have let curiosity get the better of him like that. It wasn't even the prospect of another spell in the dungeons or the stocks that worried him most. The last thing he wanted was to disappoint Gaius again.

Merlin trotted down the stairs and got himself back out in the fresh air as quickly as possible. His errands done, he realized he didn't have anywhere he especially needed to be and he thought a walk would clear his head of the unnerving incident.

He strode across the main courtyard and headed for the town, trying to focus on the fact that the sun was shining.

Ultimately, as strange as some of Lady Helen's possessions were – the doll, the book – Merlin was forced to conclude that pretty much anyone might act as suspiciously as she had if they found some stranger snooping around in their room. He had been wrong to poke about and he knew he couldn't raise the question of the doll or the book with Gaius without revealing his guilt.

The sound of traders advertising their wares woke him up to the fact that he'd wandered back into the marketplace, not far from Gaius' chambers. He began to relax a little and he started to stroll in a more casual way among the stalls.

Then he spotted Arthur with his band of friends. Up until this point his main concern had been Lady Helen, but now he wanted to make sure Arthur didn't see him.

Head down, hands in pockets, he went on his way as though he had some special purpose. He was just far enough away from Arthur to persuade himself he'd got away with it when he heard a shout that threatened to really spoil his day.

'How's your knee-walking coming along?'

He recognized Arthur's toffee-nosed voice immediately. And it was clear that he was ready for more fun at Merlin's expense . . . Merlin walked on, determined not to be drawn into Arthur's petty games. Didn't a prince have better things to do?

'Ah, don't run away.'

That was one taunt too many. Merlin stopped in his tracks.

He answered without looking back at Arthur. 'From you?'

The young prince seemed to consider this answer a cause for more teasing and so he looked at his mates to share the joke. 'Oh, thank God, I thought you were deaf as well as dumb.'

Merlin turned and faced Arthur, showing him that he was far from afraid. 'I've told you, you're an ass – I just didn't know you were a royal one.' A few guards who were loitering nearby twitched uncomfortably, several hands going for their sword hilts. Merlin continued now he seemed to have the advantage. 'What're you going to do – get your dad's men to protect you?'

Arthur grinned, setting the soldiers at ease. 'I could take you apart with one blow.'

Merlin met his grin and returned it with an

easy smile. 'I could take you apart with less than that.'

'Are you sure?'

Merlin was more than sure. He knew. The only trouble was he wasn't sure he should have boasted in that way. It was a stupid thing to have said. To think he could have been at the far end of the market already and on his way back up to Gaius. But if he left now, it would allow Arthur to win and encourage him to taunt Merlin again.

He pulled off his jacket.

Arthur laughed. His mates were really enjoying it too. Merlin decided he would just have to take their precious prince down a peg or two and see how they liked that. Then Arthur reached out and beckoned to one of his pals. The fellow handed him an evil-looking mace: a spiky iron ball dangling on a chain, strung from a stout black handle. Morning stars, Merlin knew they were called.

'Here you go, big man.' He tossed the weapon to Merlin.

Merlin fumbled and almost dropped it on his foot. It was really heavy as well as nasty. He wondered how anyone was meant to carry one into battle, let alone swing the thing. Meanwhile, Arthur had equipped himself with one too.

The prince smiled confidently and invited Merlin to make the first attack. 'Come on, then.'

Merlin stared. This couldn't be happening. He stood there, armed but not feeling very dangerous.

Arthur could tell Merlin needed some convincing. He swung the morning star above his head with the assurance of an expert. It would have been quite graceful if it weren't for the spiked ball that could cave someone's skull in. Merlin watched and decided he now had some idea of how he was supposed to use the mace.

He backed off a pace or two, still fumbling for the right grip on the handle. People were laughing and he was aware they had once again drawn a crowd. Great. This time they'd get to see him look stupid *and* also get himself killed.

Arthur stopped twirling the mace. 'I warn you, I've been trained to kill since birth.'

That was a funny line. At least, it conjured up an image for Merlin of a baby Arthur, swinging his deadly rattle as he paraded around a playpen in chain-mail nappies. Unfortunately, although the idea amused Merlin for a second or two, he soon realized this was serious.

He went for a simpler, more straightforward retort:

'Wow – and how long have you been training to be a prat?'

Arthur gave a forced, tight smile. 'You can't talk to me like that.'

Merlin nodded his understanding, making a note to pay the prince due respect.

'Sorry,' he amended. 'How long have you been training to be a prat, *my lord*?' he said, adding a mock bow.

That was the last straw as far as Arthur was concerned. He swung the mace high in the air and brought it down with tremendous force.

Merlin ducked – and prayed he'd moved fast enough.

Gaius was busy working in his chambers, mixing herbs in his bowl, when he heard the ruckus in the street below. Curious, he went to his window.

Some days he liked to look out on the general hustle and bustle of the marketplace. Today he glanced down and saw something quite different and altogether more annoying. There below him, in amongst the market stalls, he saw his young apprentice brawling with Prince Arthur. Tutting to himself, Gaius set the bowl down in despair and rushed for the door. Hunith, he thought, really should have included a warning in her letter about the headstrong nature of her son.

So far so good. Merlin had successfully ducked under the first blow and narrowly avoided the disastrous consequences of a blow to his head. But Arthur kept up his advance, whirling the mace nearer and nearer.

All Merlin could do was duck and dodge, this way and that, as he backed up along the street, always trying to keep his eye on the spiked ball and where it might fall next.

Arthur was clearly having great fun, herding Merlin along. His mates jeered and roared every time Merlin lost his footing, reminding him that, as well as keeping his eye on the ball, he ought to watch where he was going.

'Come on then, Merlin. Come on,' Arthur goaded.

Merlin staggered back, pulling himself just clear of another blow. Arthur hopped up onto a cart for some additional height and swung the mace in a playful loop, this time just missing Merlin.

Merlin thought he was out of range, but he knew it could come down on him at any time. He retreated another pace or two and brought up his own weapon to try and parry the blows.

The chain tugged unexpectedly at his arm and wouldn't move. Great: his mace had hooked itself onto the bars of a wooden birdcage hanging from a market stand. Merlin turned to wrestle it free.

Behind him he heard a clunk and as he glanced round he saw Arthur hopping off the cart to come after him. He was stuck fast there as Arthur brought the mace whistling down.

Merlin left his weapon hanging from the birdcage and dived aside to get out of harm's way. Arthur's morning star bit into a pallet of firewood, bringing the whole lot crashing to the ground. Merlin backed away, trying not to think of how easily it could have been him lying there in splinters.

Now Arthur had him at his mercy, and he wasn't sure what exactly Arthur might do. The prince was enjoying himself far too much for Merlin's liking as he came on, spinning the mace in fancy arcs, this way and that, cutting off escape to the left and then to the right, driving Merlin back more and more.

Of course, it was all a game. But as well as Arthur's obvious skill with weapons, this game relied a bit too heavily on Merlin's ability to keep out of the way.

The prince swung a blow that seemed to be aimed directly at Merlin.

Desperately Merlin threw himself backwards. His legs went up as he hit a stall and he rolled over the top. As he landed on his backside, he saw he'd just ruined a nice display of fruit, much of which was now a squishy mess stuck to the seat of his trousers.

The mace came thumping down, bashing more of the fruit and veg to a pulp – finishing off the display a treat.

At least for the moment Merlin had the stall between him and Arthur. He scrambled to his feet and moved as swiftly as he could to the right. Arthur carried straight on and vaulted smartly over what remained of the stall. He hit the ground running, eager to close up the gap.

Merlin toppled over another market stand, this one displaying animal hides. He retreated as fast as he could, watching Arthur and hoping the obstacle would slow him down. But again, he should have kept one eye on where he was going. He tripped over backwards and was flat on his bottom again, landing on a jumble of pots and sacking.

Arthur was right there, twirling the mace and closing in with a triumphant smirk. Merlin wasn't sure which he wanted to get away from more – the mace or the smirk.

He searched about him for somewhere he could

hide or something to help him. He was in a market alcove – an ironmonger's stall with metalwork and tools hanging around him and a wall at his back. He was pinned in and there was nowhere to go. Arthur was loving every second. Merlin was providing great entertainment for him and his friends.

'You're in trouble now,' the prince laughed.

'Oh, God.'

Arthur raised the mace as though for the finishing blow.

Merlin's eyes hunted around for something, anything.

Then it happened.

The crowd was still watching, but they didn't see the fire appear in Merlin's eyes. It blazed at the collection of sickles suspended from a rail above Arthur's head. Obediently they turned their blades and snatched at Arthur's flailing ball and chain. The mace became snagged in the metalwork and Arthur grimaced at his bad luck as he spun round to unhook the weapon.

Merlin was soon up on his feet and away behind another stall.

Soon Arthur had his mace freed and there was a look of even grimmer determination on his face now as he returned to his mission to deliver Merlin a hefty clout.

Merlin's eyes flared again.

This time an open-topped crate slid across Arthur's path. It sprung up as Arthur trod on one end of it and it smacked the prince hard on the shin.

'*Gaaaaaaagh!*' roared Arthur. The crowd responded with laughter.

Merlin was beginning to enjoy himself now.

Arthur swung with a ferocious blow, but Merlin moved swiftly out of harm's way and the mace smashed down on another stall, putting paid to a beautiful tray full of fresh eggs. Arthur rounded the end of the stall, aiming to cut Merlin off. Merlin ducked down the other side. Then he saw the rope trailing on the ground.

His eyes flashed and the rope stretched taut.

Now it was Arthur's turn to trip. He went flying, dropping his mace as he fell.

Merlin wasted no time. He rushed over and scooped up the weapon.

Arthur was rapidly back on his feet, but now it was him backing away as Merlin came on, having a go at twirling the morning star as best he could. Maybe it was his inexpert aim that worried Arthur the most.

'Do you want to give up?' Merlin taunted him.

'To you?' scoffed Arthur, still in retreat.

Merlin moved in, keeping up the pressure. 'Do you?'

Arthur – unaided by magic – planted his foot in a bucket and sailed over onto his back. Now Merlin really had him.

He smiled, exhilarated at the victory.

But then, just behind Arthur, he saw a face looking at him from the crowd. A stern and highly disapproving face.

Gaius.

Merlin's heart sank. He was sure nobody had seen him use magic, but he wasn't so sure the same was true of Gaius.

He felt a stab of remorse.

But that, as it turned out, was quickly replaced by a stab of hard wood in the back. Merlin whirled round, only to be rewarded with another swift jab to the gut and the sight of Arthur, very much back on his feet and meting out punishment with a broom. Arthur brought the broom up for a final, decisive smack to Merlin's face.

That was the blow that dropped Merlin to the ground like a sack of potatoes.

He lay on his back groaning and feeling the pain of bruises that seemed to cover most of his body. As he lay suffering Arthur made a show of sweeping the floor just in front of him. A few kind souls moved in to help Merlin to his feet. But no matter how kind their intentions, the way they pulled on his arms was not helping with the pain or the humiliation.

Merlin looked up and around him. Ah. The men 'helping him up' were guards. That explained it. There would be a cell waiting with his name on it.

'Wait.' Arthur motioned them aside. 'Let him go.'

Merlin blinked at Arthur, unsure if he was hearing right. He supposed he was meant to feel grateful. He couldn't tell if the young prince was showing respect for a worthy opponent or just trying to look big in front of his friends and subjects. Either way, it didn't make Merlin feel any better.

'He may be an idiot,' the prince remarked, 'but he's a brave one.' He studied Merlin for a moment, shaking his head. 'There's something about you, Merlin. I can't quite put my finger on it.'

Merlin watched Arthur go, but said nothing.

He was painfully aware of Gaius' eyes on him still.

# Chapter Twelve

Every little movement hurt and made Merlin wince with pain, and the anticipation of the scolding he was sure to get from Gaius only made him feel worse. He was surprised the old man had remained silent all the way back to his chambers, but of course Gaius would not want to take any risks. There was too great a risk of somebody catching a stray word or two and one of those words might be 'magic'. Better to stay silent. Because magic must be kept a secret, no matter what.

'How could you be so foolish?' demanded Gaius, as soon as they got inside. But it wasn't a question that expected an answer. It was just the opening line of a big lecture.

Merlin, sore all over and sore inside, wasn't in the mood. He faced Gaius' reproachful gaze defiantly. 'He needed to be taught a lesson.'

Gaius pressed on with his lecture, undeterred by interruption and entirely unconvinced by any argument. 'Magic must be studied, mastered and used for good. Not for idiotic pranks.'

'What is there to master? I could move objects like that before I could talk.' As soon as he'd said it, Merlin was aware of how much like Arthur he'd sounded: *I've been trained to kill since birth.* Such a stupid thing to say.

'Then by now you should be able to control yourself.'

Yeah, thought Merlin, and why doesn't Arthur get told to control himself? Why? Because he's the king's son? Shouldn't he be setting a better example to others?

So maybe now he knew the real reason why the king had outlawed magic. So that those in power and stuck-up prats like Arthur could throw their weight around without fear of reprisals. If he, Merlin, had been free to use magic, then that stupid fight in the street would have been over in seconds. As Arthur brandished his morning star, it could so easily have been nudged in the direction of the idiot's head. Knocked him out at the start and damaged his brain, if he had one in there.

But this wasn't about Arthur. It was about Merlin. It

was about magic. Arthur could show off his skills to everyone, but Merlin had his magic and he had to keep it hidden. He wondered if it would have been a different story if he had been born a prince instead of some poor village boy. Would the king have had his own son killed for casting spells? Merlin didn't think so.

And here was Gaius, the only person with whom he had been able to share his secret, telling him he should *control* himself. It didn't make any sense, to be born with this incredible gift and have to lock it away out of sight for ever.

'I don't want to,' he said, the confusion evident in his voice. 'If I can't use magic, what have I got? I'm just a nobody and I always will be.' Merlin caught Gaius' pained but sympathetic expression and he didn't want to be looked at like that any more. 'If I can't use magic, then I might as well die.'

Turning, he slouched off to his own room, leaving Gaius, for all his wisdom and experience, at a complete loss for words.

Merlin threw himself down on his bed and then instantly regretted such a violent move as the pain from his bruises made itself felt. He should have laid down gently.

He regretted speaking to Gaius as he just had, but he

was tired of being told he shouldn't use his magic and that he must control his powers. Merlin couldn't escape the feeling that he was right: this gift of his was part of who he was, so what was the point of it if he could never use it, never be himself?

He heard the door open and glanced up to see Gaius entering, laden with ointments, cloths, bandages and a bowl of water. If he had thought, he would have realized that the old man wouldn't leave him to sulk.

'Merlin . . .' began Gaius.

Merlin propped himself up on his elbows, determined to head off a resumption of the lecture. There didn't seem any point discussing it further unless Gaius had some answers. 'Why isn't there anyone who can help me?'

Gaius stared, stumped all over again. With all those books and all of his knowledge gained through the years he should be able to help the boy.

'Come here,' he said. 'Take your shirt off.'

Gaius sat down on the bed as Merlin grudgingly sat up and hauled off his shirt. He did his best to hide just how much it hurt. For a while he sat quietly, allowing Gaius to clean and bathe his wounds, grateful that the physician could do something to make them less painful.

'You don't know why I was born like this, do you?' Merlin asked once Gaius had cleaned most of the wounds.

Gaius stopped and held the cloth away from Merlin's back. He seemed surprised by the question that broke the silence. 'No,' he finally admitted.

'I'm not a monster, am I?' Merlin asked, trying to make the question sound like a joke. He looked at Gaius, expecting to see some kind of reaction to his words, and all he saw was a puzzled frown as he heard Gaius answer in a serious voice.

'Don't ever think that.'

Merlin was grateful for the kindness Gaius had shown him. He knew that the court physician was taking a great risk in protecting him and his special gift of magic. Merlin had probably caused Gaius more trouble in these first few days of his stay than the old man had known in all his years as the court physician. But Merlin believed that his magical powers could be used for good and his mother must have had some reason for sending him to Gaius.

'Then why am I like this? Please. I need to know – why?'

Gaius laid down the bowl and the cloth. He could only shrug.

'Perhaps someone with more knowledge than me . . .'

Merlin didn't understand this reaction. Gaius was the most knowledgeable person he had ever met.

'If you can't tell me, then no one can.' Merlin wondered if there was anyone who could help him and answer his questions. Perhaps there was no reason for him to be here with Gaius other than his mother's wishes and fears for his safety.

Gaius handed him a phial. 'Take some of this. It will help with the pain.'

As Gaius turned to leave, Merlin looked carefully at the phial in his hand, wondering if the medicine would deal with all his pains.


The candlelit dinner for two could have been quite romantic under other circumstances. As Mary Collins ate another delicious sweetmeat she began to think how different the situation might have been.

She quickly made an effort to mask the hate that she felt might be obvious in her eyes. Fortunately the man sitting opposite her seemed to have noticed no change in her expression.

This form she had stolen and the shape she had assumed managed to work its own kind of magic on him. Even a king appeared to be easily taken in by a pretty face and a winning smile. Mary Collins considered him a fool.

Once the meal was over the servants left the room and Uther and Mary were served wine by Bronwen, the young serving girl. Mary only sipped at her wine because she knew she had to stay alert and she knew if she drank too much she might offer Uther some clue to her real identity.

Uther had had enough of the servant's presence and once the girl had finished pouring him another goblet of wine he waved her away. Their table now occupied a pool of light in the middle of this big, otherwise empty room. Uther allowed a gentle smile to play across his lips.

Mary marvelled at the man's ability to hide the monster inside. They said the Devil himself could assume a pleasing shape, but he would have had a hard time competing with this man.

'Will you sing for me tonight?' Uther asked softly.

She smiled. Smiles were cheap, but the ones she crafted were art forms. 'You will have to wait, sire,' she said.

He could not hide his disappointment. 'You're not going to deny me.' There was a hint of command in his tone, as though he couldn't quite believe the refusal. Perhaps he was going to command her to sing.

'I'm saving myself for my performance tomorrow,' she teased. It had been so long since she had played these foolish games of love, but they were ways easily slipped into – as easy as slipping on a new dress. She needed to be clear on one point though. 'Will everyone be there?'

'Who would dare to miss it?'

'How about your son? It is a shame I have not yet seen him.'

That much was no lie. She had been surprised and quite genuinely disappointed not to have seen Arthur among the welcoming party. He was detained by guard duties, according to Uther, who had offered Arthur's apologies. As yet she hadn't even caught a glimpse of him going about his business in the citadel. She was beginning to believe the prince was avoiding her.

She would have really liked to see the boy. To see what a wonderful son she was going to take from Uther.

'That's Arthur for you . . .' The king gave a heavy sigh.

So Arthur had not been absent with Uther's permission. An occasional trial to his father then, like all sons. But she could also see the pride. Yes, a prince who would put responsibility for the security of the palace first before social obligations, how could a king not be proud of such a boy? But the more like Uther he was, the less trouble she would have in killing him.

'Well . . . poor child, it can't have been easy to grow up without a mother.'

This was such an easy game. So easy to steer the conversation where she wanted it to go.

Uther stiffened at the word 'mother'. As well he might.

'No,' he confessed.

Lady Helen looked at Uther with an illusion of sympathy. And if perhaps some measure of her pain had surfaced, she would claim it was the smoke from the candles stinging her eyes. 'That bond between mother and son is so hard to replace.'

Uther nodded reticently. He had no idea of how viciously barbed the remark had been. No matter: he would feel the wounds tomorrow. 'It has not been easy.'

'I'm sure. Perhaps if you found someone . . . if you remarried.' She leaned forward over the table, allowing her dark silken locks to tumble freely around her neck. 'I'm sure you would have the pick of any woman in the kingdom.'

None of her gestures were lost on Uther. Beauty was skin deep and that was as far as he saw. He smiled, enchanted. Hopeful, even.

'I might find love again.'

Mary concealed her scorn. She would see this man destroyed before that happened.

Uther roused her from her thoughts with another sigh. 'But I fear it is too late to replace Arthur's mother.'

This time it was a smile Lady Helen had to mask. How far did she dare go with her answer? He was an intelligent man, but he hadn't seen through her disguise. How blind was he?

'Yes,' she said. 'It's certainly too late for Arthur.'

Lady Helen smiled then, romance in her eyes and murder in her heart.

The king, for all his wisdom, saw only the romance.

That night, Merlin didn't bother gazing out of his window. The view of the city, with all its promise of adventure and possibilities, had lost some of its appeal. All it could offer was a collection of picturesque rooftops and spires, and they only served to remind him of his role here: a servant boy who delivered medicines to the likes of Lady Feverfew and Sir Drinksthelot. But far worse was the fact that the sight of the palace reminded him of Arthur's exalted place here.

Sleep was a long time coming. If he tossed and turned, his bruises and cuts became more painful and so he lay still. At some point he must have fallen into a deep sleep where dreams replaced the aches and pains.

*Merlin!*

The voice was speaking to him again, reverberating in his head like thunder, but also soothing like a gentle rainfall.

*Merlin!*

It seemed to become louder and Merlin expected to jolt awake to find Gaius rousing him from his bed. The voice continued to roll over him as though it was rising up through the stones.

There in the darkness, again, in some fathomless depths, he saw it: it appeared to be a flame that somehow flickered and guttered in its efforts to form a shape. Then he saw the suggestion of a head rearing up and ragged wings.

*Merlin!*

Merlin's eyes snapped open. He felt the voice vibrating through him like the tremors of an earthquake. He glanced quickly about his room. It looked just as it had when he had gone to sleep. But—

The bed, something was happening to the bed. The bed was shaking.

*MERLIN!*

The bed shook again, to the sound of his name.

Merlin sat bolt upright, listening for another call.

There was nothing. Only silence.

But he *had* heard it. *Heard it*, not dreamed it.

There was something beneath the castle – suddenly Merlin remembered Gaius' tale.

No, it couldn't be. Surely it couldn't be.

Well, impossible or not, Merlin had to find out.

# Chapter Thirteen

Out in his chambers, Gaius was snoring like a drunken ox. It was loud enough to cover a firm set of footfalls, but Merlin decided to tread softly down the steps from his room, just to be on the safe side.

Gaius was lying on his back with his mouth wide open. And as he crossed the room with gentle steps Merlin smiled at the sight of the old man so fast asleep.

He pulled on his jacket and crept carefully through the door, anxious now not to make a sound, but also keen to move quickly and track down the owner of the voice. There was no telling when it might stop calling to him and he didn't want to lose the sense of its direction.

The edge of his jacket caught on something on

the workbench and before he knew it a tin pot went clattering onto the floor.

Merlin tensed – and looked immediately at Gaius. The old man stirred and flapped an arm. Merlin could only stare, rooted to the spot. All Gaius had to do was open his eyes and he'd see Merlin there in an instant. He had no explanations to offer as to what he was doing up at this hour or where he was going.

Mumbling and grunting, Gaius shifted about a bit, then turned over onto his side and appeared to settle back to sleep. His arm had managed to push the blanket down, leaving much of his upper half exposed to the cool night air. Merlin didn't want the cold to wake him. Focusing on the folds in the blanket, the young warlock felt the surge of fire within him and he gently drew the blanket smoothly up to cover Gaius' shoulders.

With a parting glance at Gaius to reassure himself that he slept soundly, Merlin slipped out of the chamber and eased the door closed behind him.

The latch clunked rather heavily and he tensed once more. There was no sense in opening the door again to see if Gaius had stirred. He would have to press on and hope he wasn't missed. Besides, he must search for the voice and the creature that was calling to him.

Without really understanding why, Merlin was certain that the voice was for him alone. There was a special reason for its summoning him with a sound that only he could hear. Without thinking of the consequences, he was convinced he must search out the owner of the voice and discover why it called to him, why it knew his name.

Merlin's secret was safe with Gaius, but if others were to find out and he was caught he knew the punishment would be severe.

Silently and carefully, like a criminal, he stole along the corridor and crept down the stairs, half expecting a guard to come tramping round the corner at any minute.

There was no curfew and Merlin wasn't doing anything wrong by being up and about at this hour. But if he was seen, questions would be asked and he was sure his guilty look and his inability to explain himself would betray him and land him in the dungeons. Again. He listened for the sounds of any guards clad in their armour. He realized that he would be able to hear them coming well in advance.

Still trying to think of a convincing reason for wandering in the palace corridors at dead of night, he soon found himself leaving the building, and as he emerged into the night air he saw the guards patrolling on the battlements.

Just knowing the guards were there started his heart beating faster. It thumped so loudly in his ears that he was certain the sound would give him away. Telling himself not to be so stupid, he struck out across the cobbles, glancing this way and that, trying to watch all the guards at once and fearful that at any moment one of those heads could turn in his direction.

He picked up his pace to a quiet trot, hurrying into the shadows.

*Merlin!*

The voice again, ringing out like a town bell.

But nobody shouted or raised the alarm. The voice, for all its power and resonance, was clearly unheard by anyone else. Still Merlin had to trust that the voice, like his racing heartbeat, sounded only somewhere inside himself. All the same, it was unnerving when you were trying to creep about.

And the caller, like Merlin's heart, was growing more urgent, more impatient.

Feeling like a spy or a traitor, Merlin quickly looked to see where the guards were. Each one of them that he could see was occupied with their patrolling duties and it was easy for him to slip unnoticed through the entrance to the dungeons. He knew the way he needed to take, and as he went down the stairs he remembered that during the night he had spent in the dungeon he had heard the voice as though it was coming from the rocky floor of the cell. At the time, he hadn't really stopped to consider it might be real.

Now he thought back and he knew that it had *felt* real. And it felt even more real now.

Suddenly Merlin heard voices. He stood perfectly still on the staircase and listened.

Not *the* voice this time. Men. Guards. They laughed and joked, their voices turned to loud murmurs and mumbles by the echoes. There was a rattle like old bones in a cup.

Of course, the dungeons were the one place where there were sure to be guards on watch. Poking his head round the bend in the staircase, Merlin could peer down at the two guards who were sitting at a table in the hall just outside the cells.

They were playing dice.

Great. They would be settled there for an hour at least, not looking like they would be moving any time soon. *Hello, don't mind me, just passing through. I've come to see a prisoner, I can't remember his name. Oh, and actually I have to go this way, in any case, because there's this booming voice calling to me in my subconscious and I'm fairly sure it's coming from down there.* None of these lines had a chance of working, unless his aim was to get himself arrested.

Merlin had seen at a glance the arched opening opposite the entrance to the cell area. And he knew, without knowing why or how, that it was the way towards the voice. The voice was calling to him from somewhere through there.

To get to the opening he would have to cross the hall and walk right past the guards' table.

They were enjoying their game, but they weren't so absorbed in it that they'd fail to spot a stray intruder sauntering by. For all Merlin knew, they had orders to guard that entrance as well as the cells.

*Merlin!*

Merlin winced. He wanted to tell the voice, *Shhhh! I'm trying to think*.

The dice rattled again in the cup – and Merlin had his answer.

He stared, zeroing in on the dice as one of the guards tossed them out onto the table. Both men watched, awaiting their fall, waiting on the numbers.

The fire surged inside Merlin, flaring around his pupils and painting his vision with golden flame. The dice obediently carried on rolling, flinging themselves almost suicidally off the table's edge. Then they went on rolling and bouncing, clicking frantically across the cobbled floor like a couple of tiny escaping prisoners.

The guards were up like a shot, startled and surprised. One of them stood there laughing at his partner. 'Idiot, they aren't gonna roll any higher if you chuck 'em harder.'

Growling, but in good spirits, the other guard chased down the rogue dice. He bent down to pick them up. But the dice had taken a fancy to this new sport of rolling freely and they tumbled further, teasingly out of the guard's reach.

The guard grunted in frustration, then rose and hurried after them.

He stooped. They rolled away again, bouncing down the steps into the passage leading to the cells.

The other guard didn't like this turn of events. 'Hey, wait,' he called. Then he went hurrying after his comrade, before he could pick up the rogue dice. 'We play 'em as they lay. Lemme see what score you got. I ain't just taking your word for it.'

Merlin hastened past behind the guards.

'Bah,' grumbled the first guard. The dice had stopped their escape attempt, but this time the man wasn't bending to retrieve them – he was standing back a pace so his friend could get a proper look at the score.

Merlin left them to their fun and games and scampered as swiftly and as stealthily as possible to the archway.

Around the corner to the left an old wooden gate awaited him.

*Merlin!*

The voice rose up to hit him like the breath of the earth rising from deep within. The torches on the walls beside him guttered, but carried on crackling away. Merlin grabbed one from its mounting and held it in front of him. He pushed the gate gently open and stepped through.

A flight of stone stairs descended before him under a broad arched tunnel. The stones were pale and smooth, like everywhere else in Camelot, as though this might lead to a perfectly ordinary part of the citadel: a great cellar perhaps. But Merlin suspected that there was something much more exciting than rack upon rack of wine to be found down there in the darkness.

Above him in the dungeons he could hear the guards returning to their game. Already they seemed whole worlds behind him, as though they were in the past and he was venturing into the future. But then he would never have expected the future to be a place of such darkness.

Still, it was the only direction in which he could travel. Forward. And down.

It's all downhill from here, he joked to himself as he picked his way quietly down the stairs, now less fearful of getting caught by guards – but more fearful as well as curious about what lay ahead.

Somewhere, dripping water tapped out an ominous beat.

Eventually the stairs and the tunnel passed from smooth masonry to rough-hewn walls. It seemed to be either a natural passage or some old mine workings. Steep shallow steps had been crudely hacked out of the sloping floor, making Merlin's descent hard work.

He must be deep below the palace now, and the torch flames drove the shadows away before him, but as soon as he had passed they eagerly closed in behind him again. They danced like ragged demonic shapes on the bare rock walls.

The tunnel began to get narrower and seemed to squeeze in on him. The further he climbed down into the passageway, the more curious he became to see the owner of the voice.

Finally, around a bend in the tunnel, the ground seemed to level out underfoot and he emerged through a gap in the rocks onto a high ledge.

His torch flame dwindled to a tiny glow in the vastness of a cavern that seemed to go on for ever. Enormous high jagged walls rose up to a rugged domed ceiling of solid rock. Below, the walls fell away to darkness and shadow and Merlin thought he could just see a string of shapes that looked like the spine of some giant monster. Merlin craned over the edge for a better view, but his torch shed no light on the shape below.

Laughter came from everywhere at once, as though the cavern walls were amused by his arrival. Merlin wasn't happy about being laughed at by something or someone he couldn't see. He cast about, trying to pinpoint the source of the sound, and then he called into the vastness, challenging the owner of the voice to come out of hiding.

'Where are you?'

'I am here!'

Suddenly it *was* there, swooping down out of the darkness. Larger and more fearsome than he had dared to imagine, it came at him.

And Merlin knew what it felt like to be a mouse fixed in a hawk's sights and a ripe target for its talons.

# Chapter Fourteen

Merlin fought the impulse to turn and run. For one thing, he would have had to run backwards – he couldn't take his eyes off the beast. The sight of it filled him with fear.

The Dragon settled, gracefully and as easily as a bird, on the rocky mound below that Merlin had mistaken for a beast. There was a glimmer of peaceful curiosity in its huge eyes that helped to persuade Merlin that the Dragon had never intended to attack him. He supposed it just liked grand entrances.

He gazed up at the creature in awe. Even though its chosen perch was well below the ledge, the beast still managed to tower over Merlin like one of the highest walls of Camelot.

He felt the way he had the first time he saw the

king, but this time the feeling of awe and wonder was multiplied by thousands.

To be face to face with a – *the* Dragon, that was like being confronted with the impossible.

Scales shone golden and bright on its majestic crested head, all along its ridged spine and along its flanks. It may only have been the reflected torchlight, but the colours appeared to ripple with every movement of its great body. Fierce yellow eyes peered down on Merlin from under a prominent brow, forcing him to take the creature very seriously indeed.

Merlin had heard the jangling of a great chain as it flew, and as the creature rearranged itself on its mound, he could make out an enormous manacle locked around its left rear leg.

Of course, just as Merlin stared at the creature, so too the creature set to work studying Merlin.

The creature was enormous and its eyes seemed as big as moons, the pupils so broad and black Merlin wouldn't have been surprised to find stars in them. They stared without blinking at him and seemed to consider carefully before the Dragon eventually spoke with an ancient echoing voice that filled the cavern.

'How small you are . . .' the creature observed, as

though Merlin's size and feelings of insignificance needed pointing out. 'For such a great destiny.'

Merlin stood as tall and as proud as he could on the ledge, like an actor doing his best to improve his stage presence. It was no use – he still felt dwarfed by this massive Dragon.

'Why? What d'you mean?'

The Dragon made a loud roaring sound and it took a moment for Merlin to realize that the beast was laughing at him.

'What destiny?' he asked.

'Your "gift", Merlin, was given to you for a reason.'

Merlin couldn't believe it. Only today he had been asking – demanding, even – to know this one thing: what was the point of his powers, what did it all mean, what was it all for? And now the answers to those questions, that Gaius had been unable to answer, were coming from this fantastic mythical creature.

Ultimately, however amazing this meeting was, what mattered was that he was about to be told his purpose. He might have his answer.

'So there *is* a reason!'

The Dragon smiled. The baring of those great white fangs should have been a terrible sight. But it was an incredibly gentle smile for such a huge creature. The Dragon had talked, the Dragon had laughed, but that smile was the first sign that prompted Merlin to start thinking he could trust the Dragon – like he had come to trust Gaius. Merlin was eager to hear what else the Dragon had to say about him and his destiny.

'Arthur is the once and future king who will unite the land of Albion.'

It was an impressive proclamation from the booming voice, but Merlin felt the Dragon could have made anything sound important and true. And because of that sense of trust, Merlin didn't think to doubt the truth of it. Mostly he was disappointed. He had expected to hear some great revelation about himself and his gift.

Instead, here he was, having been called from his sleep and drawn down into the depths below Camelot, just to learn what a great future Arthur had ahead of him. He didn't wish to sound ungrateful, but – no, come to think of it, he did.

'Right . . .' he said uncertainly, waiting to hear how this related to him.

The Dragon ignored Merlin's lack of interest or perhaps didn't even notice as it continued to talk about Arthur. 'But he faces many threats, from friend and foe alike.'

Huh, thought Merlin. He was not surprised to hear that Arthur had enemies, even among his friends. He could understand why people didn't like Arthur. Merlin was neither friend nor enemy – how could he be? He didn't even know Arthur – but he didn't like his tormenting and bullying ways.

That Arthur was going to be king some day was certain, but Merlin wasn't sure what the 'once and future' part meant, though it sounded important. The idea of him uniting the land of Albion seemed an unlikely one given the prince's ability to annoy people. Still, Merlin was reminded that Arthur had let him off the hook after their mace fight – and he had acknowledged Merlin's bravery. That was a sign at least that he had some code of honour. Arthur might, he supposed grudgingly, make a much better king than he did a prince. Even if Merlin imagined him likely to be crowned King Prat the First.

Well, there was no point in speculating anyway, he guessed. Best to just ask.

'I still don't see what that has to do with me.'

The Dragon's head loomed closer. 'Everything. Without you, Arthur will never succeed. Without you, there will be no Albion.'

Merlin made a face.

The idea that Arthur's future depended on him, Merlin – that it was down to him to save this once and future king from his friends and foes – was just crazy. Arthur was his own worst enemy, for a start. How was he supposed to protect him from himself? To be told that his destiny was so inextricably linked to Arthur's was worse than anything Merlin could possibly imagine. Arthur was a prince and could do anything he pleased – and with authority.

He'd been begging to know his purpose in life, and this was it? Arthur was his great destiny? He shook his head. If all this were true, he hoped – no, he prayed – that Arthur had no idea what the future had in store for him. Such prophecies of greatness would only make him more insufferable than ever.

'No,' he insisted. 'No, you've got this wrong.'

The Dragon seemed to think this was mildly amusing. 'There is no right or wrong. Only what is and what isn't,' it boomed enigmatically.

Merlin was considering ways of waking himself up. Surely this was a dream. Arthur was to be a great king and Merlin was to be the one who would make it happen?

'I'm serious. If anyone wants to kill him they can go

ahead.' Actually, if it came to taking control of his own life, Merlin decided he could go one further. 'In fact, I'll give them a hand.'

More laughter, like a gentle sort of earthquake, rippled deep in the Dragon's throat. 'None of us choose our destiny, Merlin . . .' Then the tremors subsided and in their place a sadness descended, like nightfall. 'And none of us can escape it.'

Merlin could see that the Dragon had plenty to be sad about – the deaths of its fellow Dragons and its own imprisonment – but why did it feel it had to pass on this misery to others? Merlin didn't want to be involved. Why couldn't Uther and Arthur shoulder the blame? Had being imprisoned in this dark cave driven the Dragon mad?

There had to be some kind of huge mistake. The Dragon clearly knew nothing of Arthur and what he was like. Its predictions had to be wrong. How could Merlin, Gaius' apprentice, have any influence over what happened to Arthur?

'No, no way, there must be some other Arthur, because this one's an idiot.'

But the Dragon, annoyingly, had an answer for everything.

'Perhaps it's your destiny to change that.'

The Dragon stood, arching its huge back and flexing its expansive wings as though rearranging itself on its perch once more. Suddenly it kicked back with its hind legs and launched itself into the air.

Merlin watched, dismayed, as the Dragon circled higher and higher. It was doing more than merely exercising – it was leaving. Merlin held the torch high and could see the chain beginning to stretch taut as the Dragon sailed high until it disappeared into the darkness.

He searched the vaults above him desperately, watching and waiting for some glimpse of the Dragon: some sign that it was about to come flying back to him with more answers.

'Wait!' he cried out. 'I need to know more . . . !'

But this time it was only his own voice echoing around the chamber. The Dragon had gone and Merlin was left alone to work out his own destiny.

# Chapter Fifteen

Sunlight falling on his face, the sound of an opening door and someone sweeping into the room woke Merlin from sleep. He sat up – and grimaced at the way each of his bruises reminded him they were still fresh.

Memories of the night's expedition flooded in on him with the morning light. What he didn't remember was finding his way back to his bed. It had all been so incredible – his head had been so full of the encounter with the Dragon and everything it had told him, that he guessed he had probably made the return trip on instinct alone. He expected that he would take some long while trying to make sense of it all.

For now, he blinked some of the sleep out of his eyes and quickly made out the familiar shape of Gaius.

'Have you seen the state of this room?' The old man gestured incredulously.

Bleary-eyed, Merlin conducted a quick survey of the state of his quarters. Clothes scattered here and there, a few other items he recalled unpacking but had thought he'd stored somewhere more sensible than the floor. Still, it seemed a silly question on Gaius' part: of course he'd seen the state of his room.

'It just happens.'

'By magic?'

Merlin smiled at the archness of the joke. At least the subject didn't need to remain hidden between them, which was some relief. 'Yeah,' he replied, still smiling.

'Well, you can clear it up – *without* using magic.'

What did Gaius imagine he was going to do? thought Merlin. Magic some buckets and mops into action and have all the stuff stow itself away into drawers and onto the shelves? Well, it wasn't a bad idea, but no, after what he'd seen and heard last night, now wasn't the time to play games with his powers.

'Then I need you to collect some herbs,' said Gaius. Merlin blinked again. This was new. No more deliveries, but was he now expected to go foraging? 'Henbane, wormwood, sorrel – and I want you to deliver this medicine to Morgana first,' Gaius continued.

Ah, that was more like it. Gaius handed him another phial and Merlin took it while still using the other hand to rub the sleep from his eyes. He inspected the contents. Apart from the colour of the liquids, all the remedies looked alike to him.

'It's a tincture made from linden flowers. The poor girl's having nightmares.'

Merlin looked at Gaius. He wondered how much, if anything, he should tell the old man about his night's adventures. So Uther has imprisoned a Dragon underneath the castle, eh, Gaius? But no, as with the magic, now wasn't the time to be frivolous about that. Either way, he was fairly sure that whatever this poor dear Morgana was seeing in her sleep, he could beat her hands down.

'I know the feeling,' he said softly.

When Merlin arrived at Morgana's chambers, he found the door ajar. He knocked, but there was no answer. This was getting ridiculous. Did nobody around here shut their doors? Someone ought to double the guard. Just drop off the potion and go, he instructed himself. Pushing the door open, he stepped into an antechamber.

And marvelled at the sight that greeted him.

Tall and slender, Lady Morgana stood in a shimmering blue gown with her luxuriant black hair cascading down her back. She was probably about the same age as Merlin, but her refined and aristocratic features made her look older. She stood looking at herself in the mirror, ignorant of the fact that it was Merlin who had just entered her room. She was truly beautiful, he thought.

She was the lady he'd seen at the window looking at the execution. He remembered her instantly, but had scarcely imagined she could look this pretty up close.

Thankfully she was looking away from him otherwise the sudden appearance of his reflection in the mirror might have startled her. As it was, he wondered what he could possibly say, or how he could introduce himself without sounding foolish. He opened his mouth to speak and he held out the phial, still trying to think of some kind of introductory speech. 'Hello' would have been a great start, but for some reason he couldn't even manage that much right away. Before any words could emerge, she flitted away from the mirror to disappear behind a screen, still unaware of Merlin's presence.

Merlin wondered what he was supposed to do now.

'You know, I've been thinking about Arthur . . .' she said airily. As she started to undress.

Merlin blinked. He tried averting his eyes – and

failed. He had already forgotten what she'd said. Something about Arthur and hence not likely to be of interest when he was watching her gorgeous figure silhouetted against the screen. She slipped out of her gown and her bare shoulders were just visible above the screen, in beautiful pale contrast to her midnight hair.

Merlin had a hard time looking anywhere else.

Suddenly he realized that now would be a very bad time to make his introduction. Even a simple cheery 'hello' would land him in a heap of trouble. This beautiful young lady might think he was spying on her undressing. And they probably did more than put you in the stocks for that. Perhaps, he thought, the best thing would be to slip away quietly and come back later.

'I wouldn't touch him with a lance pole,' Morgana declared breezily. 'Pass me that dress, will you, Gwen?'

Merlin winced. Why did he do this, every time? If a door is open and there's no answer, knock louder, he told himself. Good advice for the future, but it wasn't going to get him out of his current fix.

Quickly he glanced around and saw the dress she must have been referring to. It was laid out on an elegant chaise longue. Quietly he hurried over and scooped up the garment to carry it to the lady. All the while he prayed she wouldn't look round.

Merlin draped the dress over the top of the screen.

Any minute now, Lady Morgana could catch sight of him and scream for the guards. He pictured himself trying to explain this to Gaius and even in his imagination he was blushing to the ears. He expected he'd have an easier time getting the old man to believe him about his night-time conversation with the Dragon.

'I mean the man is a total jouster,' Morgana continued conversationally. 'Just because I'm the king's ward . . .'

Merlin winced again. It was awkward enough to be listening in on Lady Morgana's girl talk. The fact that it was girl talk about Arthur was one more sign that he really should be going. Tentatively he started to tiptoe away, setting his sights firmly on the door and freedom.

'That doesn't mean I have to accompany him to the feast, does it?'

Merlin froze. He stood in tensed silence, praying it was a rhetorical question. It sounded like a rhetorical question.

'Well, does it?'

OK, so it wasn't rhetorical. Merlin opened his mouth.

He had to say something. His mind raced, desperately trying to think of the most non-committal answer he could offer and, more importantly, the kind of sound that would best hide the feeble attempt at a female impersonation he couldn't believe he was about to make.

'Un-uh,' he squeaked.

He grimaced at how unconvincing it sounded. Maybe it would be hidden under the convenient rustling as Morgana was busy slipping into her dress. Perhaps the screen would filter out some of the worst of it. He waited, tensed like a mouse expecting a cat's paw to strike.

Morgana shook her long locks. What on earth was wrong with Gwen's voice?

'If he wants me to, then he should invite me,' she pointed out. 'And he hasn't. So d'you know what that means?'

'Un-uh.'

Gwen did occasionally sound a bit like that when she was embroidering or attending to some sewing repairs, temporarily storing the pins in her mouth. Although why she should be doing any kind of needlework now was beyond her.

'Where are you?' She turned her head to peer over the top of the screen, to see what was ailing Gwen.

There she was, holding up the cloak in front of her. 'Here,' she piped, sounding like a mouse that had just been trodden on.

Morgana tutted. What was the girl playing at? She knew she wouldn't be wanting the cloak tonight. Morgana had a system: anything that she didn't want for that evening, she generally tossed on one of the chairs set around her table, for Gwen to put away later.

Merlin felt stupid hiding behind an upheld cloak, but it was the best cover he had been able to grab at a moment's notice. As Morgana went back to dressing, he lowered it and peered through the cloak's collar.

As feeble as the ruse was, it seemed Lady Morgana had been convinced.

'It means I'm going by myself,' Morgana said.

Merlin glanced hopefully towards the doorway. He bundled up the cloak and prepared to put it on the chair where he'd found it.

'I need some help with the fastening,' announced Morgana.

Merlin froze for the second time. Part of him would have loved to help Morgana with her fastenings.

'Gwen?' she prompted.

Merlin hunted about for inspiration, for escape. Anything.

'I'm here.'

Merlin spun round and there at the door stood Gwen. She sauntered in, but stopped as soon as she spotted him and shot him a quizzical look. Merlin was aware that this situation didn't look good. He desperately hoped their little encounter at the stocks yesterday would count for something. He quickly shot her a look of helpless appeal and showed her the phial.

Thinking quickly, Gwen recovered from her surprise and pressed a finger to her lips.

His only option was to do as he was told. He was in Gwen's hands now. She took the potion from Merlin and ushered him quickly but silently out of the room. He turned and dithered in the doorway, desperately wanting to thank her, but she gave him a smile, assuring him it could wait, as she silently shooed him on his way.

Relieved at not being caught, Merlin disappeared down the corridor and swore to himself that he would never, ever walk through a half-opened door again.

Glad to have Gwen's assistance at last, Morgana was feeling pleased with how she looked in this dark purple gown, but she needed to examine it alongside her other choice. She grabbed the other dress and waltzed to the mirror, executing a little twirl.

'So, it's whether I wear this little tease . . .' She spun

round, holding the alternative number tight to her body and presenting the full effect for Gwen's inspection. 'Or give them a night they'll really remember.'

Gwen clasped her hands together, struck silent except for a gasp of awe.

Morgana narrowed her eyes. 'Are you all right?'

'Fine, my lady. Oh, and by the way, Gaius asked me to give you this,' she said, holding up a small phial. Morgana knew only too well what that was for. She nodded and studied Gwen with friendly concern. 'Maybe you should go and see Gaius about your throat.'

'It's nothing,' Gwen insisted, smiling and touching a hand to her neck.

Morgana arched a brow, and then shrugged. Gwen sounded fine now.

Mary Collins had chosen a mustard-coloured gown for tonight's performance. It was trimmed with gold and would add a suitably spectacular splash of colour to the festivities. She didn't really think that she needed such accessories, but she was a guest of the court and must appear and behave as they expected her to. She would play their games, but not for much longer.

There was a knock at the door. Mary Collins scowled

at it as if the door itself had made the noise. She would have preferred no interruption of her preparations, but to not answer the knock would surely arouse suspicion. Adopting a courteous face, she went to open it.

At the door stood the servant girl, Bronwen, with a bowl of fruit that she handed to her with a curtsy.

'Compliments of the king,' she explained.

Mary smiled and stepped aside. 'Come in.'

Even gifts were an unwelcome intrusion, but the sooner the maid had delivered her present the sooner she would be gone. Bronwen bustled past and set the bowl on the dressing table.

Instead of leaving, the girl began to clean up the room, moving things to make everything neat and tidy. Mary endured the attention as best she could. Instead of sending the girl away, she picked up a rosy-skinned apple from the bowl. She held it under her nose a moment; the scent of the orchard was still on its skin.

'So sweet,' she said. As the maid continued with her work, she supposed some measure of conversation was called for. 'How will I ever repay him?'

There was, of course, only one way the king would be repaid. But poor Bronwen didn't need to know. She wouldn't understand. The question required no answer, but the maid was apparently a lover of chatter.

'When he hears you sing, that will be more than enough, won't it. I'm really looking forward to the performance.'

'So am I.' Mary took a bite of the apple. Under the first crunch, the flesh was soft and delightfully juicy.

'I love singing, you know. I sing all the time . . . '

As much as you chatter? wondered Mary, as she continued to bite chunks from the apple. Or perhaps the girl was simply starstruck by being in the presence of such a great singer. This Lady Helen preferred it when her 'fans' were struck dumb.

Bronwen gathered up some clothing from the corner chair, then she reached for the shawl that Mary had taken care to re-hang over the mirror after that last meddling servant had disturbed it.

'My betrothed says I have the voice of a fallen angel,' trilled Bronwen, laughing as she whipped the shawl away from the mirror, unveiling the glass. Mary hadn't noticed what she was doing and continued laughing quietly to herself at the idea of the girl's beloved comparing her to a fallen angel.

Both women stopped laughing. Both women had

turned in the same moment and gazed upon the same reflection.

The real face of Mary Collins.

Bronwen spun round and stared at Mary. Mary watched the maid's face as her poor mind struggled to make sense of the difference between what she saw before her and the face of an old hag that she had seen in the mirror. The blush had completely vanished from her young cheeks as she stared in horror.

Bronwen tried hard to pretend nothing had happened as she began to cross the room towards the door. She had to walk past Lady Helen and as she did so she made an attempt to smile. The fear of what she had seen showed clearly on her face and Bronwen was unable to hide it.

She was no actress, this maid.

Mary lashed out, latching onto Bronwen's wrist and holding her in place. Bronwen whimpered and strained against the hold, but Mary was strong and held her hand tightly so that it was impossible to move. She looked into the maid's eyes and saw the sparkle of youth turning to icy fear. Now power surged through Mary as the strength bled from the serving girl.

Bronwen buckled, collapsing to her knees. Colour flooded from her skin. Her mouth was open in a soundless scream, her breath caged in her frozen throat.

Behind her, on the dressing table, the fruit – all those lovely apples and grapes and plums – began to wither and wrinkle like dry skin, furring over and turning to stinking pulp in the bowl. All that sweetness, killed with age.

In the mirror, Mary Collins looked on, like Death watching a beautiful apprentice at work. 'Lady Helen' smiled and Death in the mirror nodded her approval.

# Chapter Sixteen

The feast was a lavish affair, and on the previous day Merlin would certainly have felt as though he didn't belong in such special company. But this evening, after his close encounter with a Dragon – *the* Dragon – everything was different. Merlin was starting to feel like he was somebody.

Of course, he was only here to serve. 'They need every available servant,' Gaius had told Merlin as soon as he'd returned from calling on Lady Morgana and collecting the herbs Gaius had requested from the market. Merlin welcomed the news. It diverted talk away from how things had gone with Morgana and it offered a refreshing change of duties. From delivery boy to waiter, it was all happening.

Merlin entered with the confident stride of someone who was on his way up in the world. Or, more importantly, someone who was hoping to get his second look at Morgana that evening. Unfortunately the first familiar face he saw in attendance was something of a disappointment.

There, waiting just inside the great hall, was Merlin's destiny. Arthur stood messing around with his friends whilst they waited for the feast to begin. Merlin watched them as they laughed and jostled each other. He thought they were behaving like a bunch of prats. Merlin felt a sagging depression. For all his humorous notions of moving up in the world, that was what lay ahead of him: a future of protecting this idiot. No thanks. Merlin drank a sarcastic toast to the future in his head.

Assuming the Dragon had been real, it must have no idea what it was telling Merlin he had to do.

Arthur barely registered Merlin looking his way. Bad form, he supposed, for a prince to acknowledge someone so lowly. All right to have a go at him with a mace, but heaven forbid Arthur should actually register his presence at a formal occasion.

Merlin cast his eyes around the room, taking in the rest of the crowd in all their fine gowns and regalia. It was quite an occasion, obviously. Long tables were arranged in a large, angular U round the room. Colourful tapestries hung all around, the grandest of them suspended behind the king's table. Candles burned everywhere, in holders carefully spaced between all the beautiful food and on high in the great candelabras that hung from the ceiling. Merlin pitied the poor guys who'd had the task of lighting those. A raised wooden dais – a stage – dominated the far end of the room. The guests, decked in all their richest finery, milled about and mingled between the tables. All Merlin could hear was the babble of competing conversations and murmured anticipation.

Suddenly Arthur blurted out, 'God have mercy!'

He was staring towards the entrance to the hall – and he and his friends had suddenly stopped their noise and horseplay and joined in the ogling. Merlin turned to see what they were gawping at . . .

. . . and gawped right along with them. His heart was suddenly in his throat and his jaw on the floor.

Lady Morgana. Stunning the whole party into silence, it seemed; either that, or Merlin had simply gone deaf to everything else around him. She looked supremely elegant in a wine-coloured dress which was halter-necked to leave her shoulders bare and drawn in at the waist by the most elaborate golden belt fashioned in the shape of leaves. A golden collar and a beaded headband, like the slenderest of crowns, set the outfit off in a truly regal manner. She tossed easy smiles around the hall, like dishing out hand-outs to the poor. She was clearly aware of everyone's attention on her, including Arthur's, but Arthur was one person she never looked at directly.

Merlin liked her even more.

'Merlin!' snapped Gaius.

'Mmm?' Merlin half turned his head. Only half, so he could keep an eye on Morgana.

'Remember – you're here to work.'

Merlin rolled his eyes: how could he forget? Keeping his sigh to himself, he picked up a tray of drinks from the side table and set off to serve the guests. By and large though, they had to help themselves from his tray, since his eyes were constantly on Morgana. He wished he had the courage to go closer to her and maybe even offer her a drink, but then he noticed she already had a goblet in her hand. He had faced Dragons, so facing a princess should be no problem he thought.

Gwen came up unexpectedly on his left. 'She looks great, doesn't she?'

'Yeah.' Merlin nodded a bit too eagerly.

'Some people are just born to be queen.'

Merlin felt like he'd been struck with a missile from a catapult. He'd already thought of Morgana as out of

144

his league, but as a queen-in-the-making she was even further beyond his reach. 'Really?'

'I hope so. One day.'

Merlin looked at her, mildly dubious. Did she think serving a queen was any higher a position than serving the king's ward? Well, maybe it was. But with Gwen, she seemed so sweet-natured and good-hearted, it was possible she only wanted Morgana to become queen because she liked the woman.

'Not that I'd want to be her,' Gwen added. 'Who'd want to marry Arthur?'

'Not me,' agreed Merlin. Briefly he searched around for Arthur. There he was, still larking about and playing at being more important than everyone else. Then Merlin looked again at Morgana. She was so beautiful. Was she really doomed to marry Arthur? The poor girl. Talk about a damsel in distress.

Gwen got busy handing out drinks. Merlin followed her example and to break up the monotony of waiting on the lords and ladies he began to gently tease her.

'Oh, come on, Gwen, I thought you liked those "real rough, tough, save-the-world kind of men".'

'No, I like much more ordinary men, like you.'

'Gwen, believe me, I am not ordinary.' He was

feeling far from ordinary today. Even less ordinary than usual. How many people around this room, for all their riches and trinkets and royal blood or whatever, could say they had met a Dragon last night? Yeah, figured Merlin; that made him really special.

'I didn't mean *you*!' said Gwen, clearly feeling the need to clarify. She fought down her blushes. 'Obviously not you. But just, you know, I like very ordinary men, *like* you.'

Suddenly they were back at the stocks again, with Gwen putting her foot in it. It was fun though and Merlin got as much out of it as he could.

'Thanks.' He played up his wounded expression and waited for Gwen to take the bait. It didn't take long.

Mary Collins sat at her dressing table, putting the finishing touches to her outfit and making sure she looked perfect as Lady Helen. The guests would be expecting her soon. Or rather, they would be expecting Lady Helen.

She had affixed a rather grand collar of lacy blue fabric to her dress, lending it an extra theatrical air. She fingered the amber pendant that hung on its chain about her neck, singing lightly to herself – and feeling the sound of her song resonate within the stone. Satisfied, she dropped the stone to rest, hidden away by the folds of fabric at the front of her dress.

She stood and moved towards the door, passing Bronwen's lifeless corpse on the floor. There would be no need to get rid of the body. Let them find it. They would have sharper sorrows to deal with by then and Mary Collins would be no more.

Besides, her audience was waiting.

Morgana took her seat, pleased with the entrance she had made. A party was a party, after all, and some things were worth doing right, no matter what the occasion. Besides, despite her earlier misgivings, she was genuinely looking forward to Lady Helen's performance. It promised to be a rare treat.

Failing that, she had faithful company in the form of Bruno, one of Uther's hunting dogs who had chosen to nuzzle in beside her legs and wait for whatever scraps happened to fall from the table. Morgana studied the animal's plaintive expression, wondering how long he had been practising that look. He was very good at it. Patience, she told the dog silently. She picked up a piece of chicken from her plate and surveyed the gathering, waiting for an opportune moment to slip him a tasty snack. The dog whimpered pitifully. Morgana felt someone brushing past behind her and instinctively she knew it was Arthur.

He leaned in to speak to her. 'Oh, I didn't see you arrive, Morgana.'

Morgana smiled to herself. Everyone had seen her. Arthur might be a master swordsman, but when it came to verbal fencing she could hold her own. 'I didn't notice you were here or I would've come over, Arthur.' She dropped her gaze to the large hound who was now sitting up, licking his chops and eyes practically watering at the sight of the chicken in her hand. So close – and yet so tantalizingly out of reach. She twirled the chicken lightly before taking a nibble. Then she handed it to Bruno and he snapped it up gratefully and settled back down under the table, munching away happily.

Morgana glanced over her shoulder, expecting Arthur to still be there, but he had already taken his seat at his father's side, leaving their little duel for now. Point to her, she decided. Not the most impartial of umpires, maybe, but it was more fun that way.

Just then the room fell quiet as the conversation fizzled out all along the tables. Morgana was reminded that there was better entertainment than annoying Arthur and so she dabbed at her lips with the napkin and settled back to listen.

Uther Pendragon passed his gaze all around the guests, as though to favour everyone with a visit from the royal countenance. Then he addressed the assembly.

'We have enjoyed twenty years of peace and prosperity. This has brought the kingdom and myself many rewards and pleasures, but few of them as great as the honour of introducing the beautiful and wonderful Lady Helen of Mora.' As he spoke he gestured towards the far end of the room.

Lady Helen was standing ready on the small stage, ready to outdo Morgana's entrance. She waited for the applause to fade. Nothing must break the spell of her first note.

Silence. The hall belonged to her.

She lifted her head and began to sing in the ancient tongue. The words were less important than the notes they struck, but she sang of loss, and of the loneliness of one soul robbed of another. She spread her hands, feeling the first breath of a breeze finding its way into the hall, the gentle current like ghosts answering the call of her song. She saw them toy with the candle flames, but nobody else noticed the flickering light.

All eyes were on her. All their thoughts were hers.

She raised her arms, gesturing with open palms as though massaging the notes as they hung in the air. Sending them on their way down the hall to do her bidding.

Slowly, gracefully, she stepped down from the stage, ushering the notes of her song, like spirits, ahead of her.

Merlin could feel Lady Helen's voice filtering into him, flowing through him like his own blood. Haunting, cold, beautiful, it blew like a wind across unknown lands. A dreamscape opened up before him, calling upon him to explore.

As Lady Helen moved off the stage, she advanced with a kind of drifting, swaying motion, like a cloud might dance if it could. Merlin felt his head begin to sway along with her, like a baby being rocked to sleep. Yes, sleep.

No.

He blinked and shook his head. What was happening?

Lady Helen raised her voice, filling the room with crystal-clear notes, high and pure, and Merlin saw heads beginning to loll all along the tables. Cold gusts now blew through the room, whipping between the diners and snuffing out the candles, consigning the hall to shadow and darkness.

In the darkness, wisps of smoke curled towards the ceiling, dancing to the tune of Lady Helen's song.

She advanced, her voice rising in a steady crescendo.

More and more people succumbed, their heads tilting and tilting until finally they toppled, people falling back in their chairs or slumping forward over the table, making pillows of their folded arms.

Merlin clamped his hands over his ears. He glanced this way and that, seeing only more and more falling under the spell. Gaius. Morgana. Arthur. The king. Nobody was immune.

Even Merlin could still hear her song, probing between his fingertips as though trying to worm its way into his ears. He held his hands tight to his head, straining to think of something, anything, to fence it out and keep himself awake. He thought at first of the Dragon, but that led him back to magic and the enchantment of the song all around him.

He thought instead of all the names he had given to Gaius' patients. Lady Feverfew. He hadn't seen her among the guests tonight. Sir Casper Buckbean. Master Henry Wormwood. And – and – stupid, ordinary things. Over and over, to shut out the magic.

In the dying light, as the guests surrendered to sleep, he could see another change taking place. In line with Lady Helen's procession, cobwebs knitted their way over the diners. Fruit and other food on the tables furred with mould and turned to mush. This was more than sleep: this was like time creeping over the slumbering guests and stealing away their lives. Webs coated everything, feather-light and silver-white like an old woman's hair.

Everyone lay buried in a fine lace of age.

With her audience unconscious, in their soulless sleep, Lady Helen's advance grew darker and more sinister. Her arms raised in exultation, she moved like some Angel of Death. Hatred filled her eyes and she clenched her teeth and seemed to spit the notes out like a snake spits out venom.

Closer and closer she came, moving carefully and slowly towards the king's table. Merlin looked from her to the table – and back again. He realized her eyes were targeted on the sleeping Arthur.

Her hand slid to her left sleeve and plucked forth a shining dagger. She raised it and her song was practically a scream.

Lady Helen truly was an Angel of Death. Arthur, defenceless and oblivious, sat with his head lolled back and his eyes closed. A powerless victim, waiting for death to strike.

# Chapter Seventeen

Suddenly Merlin could see things in a new light. However much he had argued against the Dragon's predictions, suddenly there was a life at stake.

It didn't matter what he'd told the Dragon.

It didn't matter that Arthur was a bit of an ass.

He didn't deserve to die.

Merlin had to act. Pure and simple as that.

But what to do? He glanced about, hunting for something, anything he could do.

The songstress had no such trouble. She had one single purpose. A son for a son. The dagger flashed in her hand, drawn back further for the fatal blow. Aimed at Arthur's heart.

Something prompted Merlin to glance up towards the ceiling.

Without a second thought, his instincts latched onto

the chandelier – and his gaze flared with the familiar fire. His heart thumped loudly in his ears, deafening, lending the flames a galloping rhythm. Unseen energies lanced out at the heavy chain suspending all that heavy wood and wrought iron from the ceiling.

With a loud explosion, one of the links snapped. Wood and iron, candle wax and flame. It seemed to take an age to fall as time itself slowed for Merlin.

Its slow fall allowed Lady Helen the chance to glance up as she heard the chain link snap. The dagger was still in her hand, but the purpose fled from her eyes. In rushed fear, horror, anger, despair, defeat.

Then time was free to flow forward at its customary pace. Lady Helen barely had a moment to throw up her arms and cry out as the chandelier came crashing down on top of her. Crushing her voice, killing her song, and pinning her to the floor.

Merlin breathed a sigh of relief. For a while, he seemed like the only living thing in the room. And then, in the silence, the guests steadily began to stir under their blankets of cobwebs. Senses dulled, they were slow to wake, then they began flicking and swatting irritably at the silky mesh of cobwebs that had held them fast and covered them. Fully awake, they were glancing about in a panic, probably on the lookout for the spiders responsible for it all. Merlin stood perfectly still, unable to take his eyes from the broken figure crushed under the weight of the chandelier.

'In God's name, what's happened here?'

Merlin started at the sound of the king's voice. Naturally the king would be among the first to recover his senses. And he had missed the main part of the show along with everybody else. All he would know was what he could see in front of him, and what he could see was his honoured guest squashed under the great chandelier.

At least Merlin hoped they couldn't put the blame for this on him. Then he thought: they might. That was the way things had happened here at Camelot so far.

Cautiously Arthur stood and leaned forward over the table, frowning at the form pinned to the floor in front of him. His grimace was mirrored by many faces around the room. In Uther's eyes there was terrible recognition.

Merlin looked again, this time properly.

There, wrapped in Lady Helen's mustard-coloured gown, was the lined and twisted figure of an old woman. Not just any old woman: the ancient, withered woman Merlin had seen at the execution. The mother of Thomas Collins. Struggling, her legs still hopelessly pinned – and probably crushed – behind her, she lifted her upper body onto her hands and raised her wizened face.

Her movements were jerky and fitful, but as Merlin watched, murder flashed once more in her eyes. The dagger was still clutched in her hand. With a last rasping breath, like the hiss of a dying snake, she hurled the blade with a force that would have put the strongest young knights to shame. She collapsed, her work done – and her life spent. The dagger spun, end over end, on its way to Arthur's heart.

There was no time to do anything.

Burning gold ringing his eyes, Merlin *made* time.

Once again, everything slowed.

The dagger was there, flying at Arthur's chest. All eyes seemed fixed to it and its target. Arthur was poised to dive, one way or another, but his indecision would cost him his life.

Merlin, free to move at normal speed, dived at Arthur. His arms out, he struck the prince hard and dragged him down. They fell to the floor together, Merlin banging his shoulder against the stones.

Somewhere behind Merlin's left ear, there was a thunk – like something metal taking a bite out of wood. Together, Merlin and Arthur looked to see the knife sticking out of the back of Arthur's chair like a large pin marking his position at the table.

Arthur stared, breathless. At the knife. Then at Merlin.

A rousing cheer erupted around the table. There were hands clapping, and as Merlin scanned some of the faces of the guests it dawned on him that they were all looking in his direction.

Nearby, the king himself moved into view. Crossing to the chandelier on the floor, he stared down at the crumpled figure at his feet. Disbelief crystallized in his eyes.

Morgana stood at Uther's side. She was stunned and horrified by what little she had seen. She was no different from anyone else in the room in that respect, but she wondered now whether she might be the only one who felt at all sorry for the old lady. She studied Uther's bowed head and wondered if he was remembering what she had told him the night after the execution of Thomas Collins: '*The more brutal you are, the more enemies you'll create.*' In case he wasn't thinking of her comment, she leaned closer to him and murmured, 'I warned you.'

He glared at her, but said nothing. He was probably reluctant to waste valuable anger on her.

Most of it would be reserved for the dead woman on the ground.

Merlin wasn't much of a lip-reader, but he noticed that no matter the exact words Lady Morgana had uttered, they had earned her a sharp look from the king. If she was to be queen some day, Merlin fancied it wouldn't be with Uther's blessing. Not today anyway.

Arthur hauled himself up from the floor. Merlin too got up on his feet. They looked at each other, but were both stuck for anything to say.

King Uther saved them the trouble. He strode over and laid a paternal arm round Arthur's shoulders, as though wishing to assure himself that his son was warm and real and very much alive. His kingly gaze was on Merlin, however.

Uh-oh, thought Merlin. Here it comes. Dungeon time again. Although he couldn't quite say why.

'You have saved my boy's life,' Uther told him. 'A debt must be repaid.'

Merlin shifted from foot to foot. 'Uh, well . . .'

The king appeared impatient with his blushes. 'Don't be so modest. You shall be rewarded.'

Grinning, despite himself, Merlin was unsure of the proper etiquette here. He decided to err on the side of caution and continue with the modesty.

The king was unlikely to clap him in the stocks for being coy.

'No, honestly . . . you don't have to, your highness.'

Or should it have been 'your majesty'? Merlin winced inwardly. Maybe he'd gone and put his foot in it anyway. The king let the faux pas pass unnoticed. His mind was made up.

'Oh, absolutely, this merits something quite special . . .'

'Well . . .' When it came down to it, Merlin was not going to quarrel with a king.

An idea sprang to the king's mind. 'You shall be rewarded with a position in the royal household.'

Wow. Merlin stood a little taller, a smile spread right across his face.

'You shall be Prince Arthur's manservant.'

Cheers went up, filling the great hall to the ceiling.

Merlin's eyes met Arthur's. Arthur's crestfallen expression mirrored his own. Apparently they were in agreement on something at last.

'Father!' protested Arthur.

That was the key difference. Arthur could complain, while Merlin had to quietly accept his 'reward' and put up with it.

Across the hall, Merlin could see Gaius smiling and applauding with the rest of the guests. And there was Gwen and even old Sir Drinksthelot, although he didn't look entirely like he knew what was happening. Everyone was cheering Merlin.

Now he really could feel he was somebody.

Although when it came to being a somebody, Arthur's manservant would have come fairly low down on his list of choices.

# Chapter Eighteen

Wow, was the most coherent thought that came to Merlin's mind for some time after the events in the great hall. Of all the possibilities he had hoped for when he had looked out over the city of Camelot the first night he had arrived, this had never occurred to him. Not once, not ever. He had a real position in the court now.

Later when he was alone in his room, he had his first opportunity to make sense of it all. But he was still puzzled by the events and the Dragon's words. He sat leaning against a bench that stood just under the window. In the absence of any other focus, his gaze rested on the candle flame in front of him. He watched it tremble and flutter, unable to hold a constant shape, bowing to the slightest breath. Was that how it was for him and his gift? His magic felt so much like a fire within him, but was it subject to as many whims and breezes as the candle. Was that his fate? To be blown this way and that?

Or perhaps these latest events, odd though they were, could be the first steps along a much more interesting path. A start to the so-called destiny the Dragon had prophesied for him. It had told Merlin that his fate was destined to be linked with Arthur's, but had Merlin had any idea that was going to be as servant and master, well, he might have raised even louder protests. Or maybe he wouldn't. He just needed to see how things were going to work out.

A knock at the door snapped him out of his thoughts of the future and he turned, wondering if life had more surprises to throw his way.

It was Gaius with an object wrapped in red cloth tucked under one arm. He wore a wry smile, as though he had caught something of the buzz of thoughts in Merlin's head. He stopped in front of the bench, hugging the bundle to his chest.

'Seems you're a hero,' he said.

For all his weightier thoughts on the subject, Merlin could still see the joke. 'Hard to believe, isn't it?'

'No,' Gaius assured him in earnest. 'I knew it from the moment I met you.'

Merlin laughed. Now that was a good one. Whatever he had looked like when he had first shown up, he knew for certain he hadn't looked like your average hero.

'You saved my life, remember.'

That sounded too grand a way of summing up what had only amounted to averting a nasty fall. It didn't strike Merlin as being in the same league as steering Arthur clear of a dagger's path. Besides, the two were totally different situations – or should have been, as far as Gaius knew.

'But . . . that was magic.'

Gaius nodded, changing the nature of his smile to something keener, and more knowing. 'And now it seems we've finally found a use for it.'

'What d'you mean?'

'I saw how you saved Arthur's life.'

'No.'

'Perhaps that's its purpose,' insisted Gaius.

Merlin relented. He guessed there was no use denying it any more. At least, if someone had to see he had used magic to save the prince, then it was a blessing it had been Gaius. Had anyone else witnessed it and recognized his use of magic for what it was, well, Merlin would have been straight back in those dungeons instead of sitting here talking with a friend.

So, if there was no sense in denying it, was there any sense in fighting the Dragon's prophecy? Well, he didn't know if he was quite ready to go along with everything the Dragon had said, but perhaps saying it out loud might draw unwanted attention to his magic powers.

'My destiny,' he observed.

'Indeed.' Gaius, bless him, preferred to take it seriously.

Shaking such matters aside for the moment, the old man appeared to remember the bundle. He stepped forward and presented it to Merlin. The artefact hidden inside the crumpled red cloth intrigued him immediately, not least because this was one of the first things Gaius had handed him that wasn't a phial. He regarded it dubiously for a second, worried that it might be a *box* of phials to be delivered to some poor sufferer in Camelot. That would be quite a parting gift: one last major delivery round.

Still, the glint in Gaius' eye seemed to indicate otherwise, and in any case he was there holding the object and waiting for Merlin to take it from him. Merlin stood and stretched out his hands to take the gift.

'This book was given to me when I was your age,' Gaius explained, 'but I've a feeling it will be more use to you than it was to me.'

Merlin took it gratefully and was surprised by the weight of it in his hands. A book that heavy had to contain matters of real substance. Eagerly he unfolded the cloth to uncover a volume bound in brown leather and sealed with intricate metal clasps. A diamond design crafted in brass and set with a single jewel dominated the centre of the cover.

Suddenly Merlin knew with a tingling certainty what kind of matters the book contained. And he was reminded of the question he'd put to Gaius, about whether he had ever studied magic. He was stunned at the idea that Gaius would have been given a book of magic when he was young. Gaius must have grown up in a very different age to this one. Merlin was impressed that, despite the dangers, he had kept the book and was now passing it on to him.

The book reminded him too, in some respects, of the book he had seen in Lady Helen's chambers. This one was grander and more impressive, but it carried the same sense of power with secrets locked between its covers.

'A book of magic . . .' He grinned in delight.

'Which is why you must keep it hidden,' Gaius said seriously.

Suddenly Merlin remembered the withered features of Mary Collins, and the man he had seen executed on his first day in Camelot. That was where these kinds of secrets could lead anyone who wasn't careful. A chilling image of his own mother crying out in the courtyard as the axe robbed her of her son passed through his imagination. He ushered it quickly on its way.

That wasn't a possibility he wanted to think about. Not now.

It was a warning, yes, and he would be cautious. But if there was any destiny at play at all then it was here, in this act of Gaius giving him this book.

Merlin couldn't wait to get stuck in, unfastening the clasps and leafing through the pages. Arcane symbols and texts, drawings and runes flicked past in a dazzling and mystifying array. His eyes raced over the writings as he eagerly went from page to page. Just like his thoughts about his destiny and the Dragon's words, he could make very little sense of things he saw on the pages. But it was a beginning.

The possibility of answers. That was what this book offered to him.

He looked at Gaius. This was the best gift ever. He

held the book in his hands feeling the heavy weight of it. 'I will study every word.'

He was about to say 'thank you' to Gaius for such a superb present when there was a loud knock at the door. Both Merlin and Gaius looked up: who could it be now?

'Merlin! Prince Arthur wants you right away!'

The gruff voice of a guard ordered him to go immediately. Typical Arthur. Only he could send someone to fetch him at the most inconvenient time. Well, he supposed, that was a prince for you.

Gaius smiled at Merlin.

'Your destiny's calling. You'd better see what he wants.'

Merlin returned the grin. He'd gone from running errands for the court physician to running errands for the crown prince of Camelot. Some people would call that quite a promotion. Merlin knew Arthur though, and he knew it might just as easily be a step in the wrong direction.

# Epilogue

Deep in the shadows of its cavern, the Great Dragon cared little for the daily comings and goings in the citadel above. The passage of a thousand people traipsing the corridors and courtyards of Camelot went unheard, day after day.

But Merlin – Merlin was different. The slap of his footsteps on stone as he ran to his new master was like the beat of a young Dragon's wings, always audible no matter how distant. The Dragon mourned for the sound it would never hear again, but it enjoyed hearing the running footsteps of the boy with a destiny before him.

One was the past, unreachable.

The other was the future.

But no longer would every step be an adventure for Merlin. The boy had learned a little of the more humdrum facets of a life's journey – duty, responsibility, work. Many more lessons lay ahead.

He had saved young Arthur's life once, but that was only the beginning. The young man had shown himself a hero, but there were many more things to learn and many more adventures ahead of him. This was only the first step on the road of his destiny.

# Also Available

# Valiant

Text by Mike Tucker

Based on the story by Howard Overman

Continue the adventures at **bbc**.co.uk/**merlin**

# Chapter One

The storm bore down mercilessly on the hillside town. Dark, swollen clouds raced across the sky like black wolves, obscuring the pale moon that struggled to rise in the sky and turning evening into night. Fat raindrops started to fall, slowly at first but with gathering momentum until the ground was sodden and slick.

Villagers hurried for houses which stood huddled beneath the shelter of the forest, as fingers of lightning danced and crackled above the treetops and thunder echoed around the valley below. Smoke from a dozen or more chimneys was snatched up by the wind and sent spiralling away like pale wraiths searching for victims.

Robert Mayer cursed under his breath as a gust of wind caught the awning over his stall, whipping it back and sending water cascading over the meagre display of vegetables that he had on show. Market day here was rapidly becoming a disaster as fewer and fewer people bothered to make the long trek up from the valley below. This storm would do nothing to help matters. He had only just sold enough to cover the feed for his horse. It had barely been worth the effort of setting up shop at all.

With a weary sigh of resignation he started to untie the rain-soaked awning. There was no chance that he would sell anything more today, perhaps next week would be better.

A noise made him turn. A figure on horseback emerged from the swirling tendrils of wood smoke, a dark cloak pulled tight around his head and shoulders. The horse's hooves clacked on the wet cobbles of the street. Villagers rushed past, heads bowed against the rain. Strangers rarely came to this place, and when they did no good ever came of it.

Robert Mayer watched as the horseman rode slowly down the main street. He stopped at a tangle of shabby wagons and hastily erected stalls that formed the market. Stallholders hurried to bring in goods from the driving rain and lash down awnings that flailed in the strength-ening wind.

The horseman slid from his mount, securing the reins to a low post. He turned and looked at Mayer.

'You there,' he called. 'Where would I find Devlin?'

Mayer gave a snort of disgust. Devlin. Strangers, when they came, always came for Devlin. The village should have kicked out that shabby excuse for a sorcerer a long time ago. He spat into the mud and busied himself with his stall.

'Do I look as though I have time to give directions?'

'No,' said the stranger. 'You look like a fat, insolent peasant with no manners who needs to be taught a lesson.'

Mayer turned, his face flushing and anger rising in his chest. 'You will regret that.' He reached for the heavy mallet at his belt, striding through the mud towards the man who had insulted him.

There was a flash of steel and a sword blade sliced through the driving rain, coming to rest at Mayer's throat. The stallholder gasped in pain as the sword's tip pierced his skin.

The horseman pulled at the ties of his cape, letting it drop open. Mayer's eyes widened as he glimpsed the armour and colours of a knight of the realm.

'Forgive me,' stammered Mayer. 'I did not know . . .'

The knight smiled, but it wasn't a pleasant smile.

It was more of a sneer. A tall man with close-cropped hair and piercing grey eyes, he held himself like a warrior, tense, poised, always watching. He might have been described as handsome once, but the skin of his face bore the signs of too much time spent on the battlefield, and there was something about the set of his jaw, the curl of his lip, that gave his face a cruel edge and said that this was not a man to be trifled with.

He watched with amusement as a rivulet of blood trickled down the length of his glistening sword blade, then he turned to Mayer, fixing him with a piercing stare.

'Well, now you do know.' The knight twisted the tip of his sword and Mayer winced in pain.

'Please, Sir . . .'

'Valiant.'

'Sir Valiant. I meant no disrespect.'

'Really? Then I'll ask you again. Where will I find Devlin?'

Mayer pointed a trembling finger towards the far end of the market. 'His is the last stall, at the far end of the street.'

The knight removed his sword from Mayer's throat, wiping the blood from the blade with the edge of his sodden cloak. 'Tend to my horse, and be quick about it. I do not intend to be here long.'

'At once, sir.'

Mayer watched the knight stride purposefully through the tangle of stalls, villagers moving to get out of his way. He touched the wound at his throat. He had been stupid, and was lucky to escape with his life. It was always the same when strangers came to see Devlin – each time they brought trouble with them.

'We really should have kicked him out years ago,' he growled.

As Valiant made his way through the market, he smiled to himself – there was nothing quite like the livery of a knight to strike fear and awe into the hearts of peasants.

The stalls at the far end of the village were clustered more closely together than at the other end, their wares displayed less prominently. Dim firelight guttered in heavy torches. Valiant could see strange runic symbols, pentagrams and other mystical paraphernalia being hurriedly hidden from view as he passed.

Small wonder. These people were dicing with death by buying and selling occult items so openly. If Uther Pendragon knew of their trade . . . But then, if Uther

Pendragon knew that a knight of the realm was here amongst them and what he intended to do . . . Valiant gave a snort of amusement. The king would never know.

He pushed aside a line of sodden blankets hanging across the street. Through the wood smoke and driving rain he could see the stall that the stallholder had described, a collection of rickety tables and hastily assembled shelves huddled within the crumbling stone walls of a disused building. Heavy canvas had been strung from the building's roof to try and give some shelter from the downpour. Valiant pushed aside the fabric with the tip of his sword and slipped inside.

The interior was dark and laced with the aroma of unfamiliar herbs and strange spices, but it was warm and dry, and despite the distaste he felt being in this environment, Valiant was grateful to be out of the storm.

He peered past the jumble of strange-shaped objects that hung from the tent poles and lay in untidy piles on tables. At the rear of the tent he could see a lone figure hunched over a flickering brazier.

Devlin.

The sorcerer looked up as Valiant stepped into the firelight, then he bowed his head.

'Sir Valiant.'

'I understand you have a shield for me.'

Devlin nodded and gestured towards a shrouded shape resting on a table near the fire. He crossed to the table and with a flourish flung back the cloth.

Valiant stared. The shield itself was nothing special, a gentle curve of burnished steel, the handle on its back held in place with leather straps, but the design that was painted upon its surface . . .

Three serpents coiled and writhed across the shield's face, every scale on their bodies painted in exquisite detail. The three mouths, gaping wide, revealed wickedly pointed fangs, their tips dripping with venom, while the eyes of the snakes glared malevolently. It was a shield designed to strike fear into the hearts of those who faced it.

Valiant reached out with a gloved hand but Devlin caught his wrist and gave a shake of his head. 'I wouldn't, sire. The serpents of the Forest of Balor have the deadliest of venom. With your swordcraft and this shield, I guarantee you victory.'

Valiant shook himself free of the sorcerer's grasp.

'Show me how it works.'

Devlin stretched out his hands towards the shield. He took a deep breath and started to mutter – deep, guttural, unfamiliar words. His eyes rolled backwards in his skull, their whites glinting in the firelight.

With a sudden hiss of anger the snakes erupted from the surface of the shield, their black, sinuous bodies bulging free from the metal, their tails still part of the metal surface, their heads bobbing and weaving as they searched for their prey.

Valiant took an involuntary step backwards, sword raised. These were like no snakes he had ever seen before. These were ancient, deadly things of myth.

Devlin watched with amusement as Valiant stared, transfixed by the writhing snakes.

'When you are competing in the tournament, you pin your opponent under the shield and then' – he stabbed two fingers towards Valiant's face – 'a snake strikes! Your opponent will be paralysed in seconds!'

Valiant nodded, still keeping his eyes on the snakes. The shield was better than he could have hoped for. A frown flickered across his brow.

'How do I bring the snakes to life?' he questioned. 'I don't know magic.'

Devlin raised his hands again. 'You don't need to know magic, sire, I will enchant them for you.'

He intoned the harsh, unfamiliar words of the old magic once more and the snakes' frantic hissing calmed, their heads slowing then no longer straining to reach Valiant.

Devlin turned and bowed. 'The snakes are now under your command. They will do anything you tell them to do.'

An unpleasant smile flickered at the corner of Valiant's lips. 'Anything?'

'Just say the word.' Devlin grinned, revealing yellowing, crooked teeth.

Valiant stepped back, pointing at the sorcerer. '*Kill him!*' he snapped.

Devlin's smile was still on his lips when the first snake lunged at him, sinking its fangs into the flesh of his neck. The scream had barely started to build in his throat when the two remaining snakes joined in the attack.

Robert Mayer watched as the cloaked knight swept out of the village in a flurry of spray. As the sound of hoof beats faded into the night, he made his way through the deserted market to the stall of Devlin the sorcerer. The entire village had heard the scream, but somehow it had fallen to Mayer to go and see what had happened. Gingerly he drew aside the flaps covering Devlin's stall and peered into the dim interior.

Devlin lay sprawled across the earthen floor, his face frozen in an expression of pure terror, his hands outstretched towards some unseen horror.

Mayer shook his head. He had disliked the sorcerer, but this was no way for a man to die. It was as he had said, nothing good ever happened when strangers came asking for Devlin.

Valiant rode through the night, the shield strapped securely to his arm. As the storm started to fade and early rays of light began to creep above the hills, he caught his first glimpse of his destination.

The vast castle spread out across the hillside. Flags and pennants fluttered from every tower, vivid and proud against the pale morning sky. Hundreds of buildings nestled within the protective walls, bathed in the light reflected off the gleaming white stone.

Spurring his horse onwards, Valiant entered the city gates, purposefully moving through the throng of horses, knights and officials that had started to gather for the tournament. He always liked to make an impression when he entered a city for the first time and his jet black horse and billowing, mustard-yellow cloak were already attracting attention. By keeping his helmet on he also conjured a sense of unease.

Eager servants hurried forward to steady his horse as he dismounted. Valiant barely acknowledged them. He strode across the field where the visiting knights were congregating at the desk of the steward, and stood impatiently as a competing knight clad in the colours of one of the eastern countries was registered by the court official.

'Store your amour and weapons in the armoury and report back here for the opening ceremony at nine o'clock tomorrow morning,' the official said finally.

The eastern knight nodded, then turned to leave, acknowledging Valiant with a curt bow of his head.

The steward looked up expectantly. Valiant lifted off his helmet and brought it down hard on the desk, making the official jump. With a humourless smile Valiant presented his colours: three black snakes on a blaze of yellow.

'Knight Valiant of the Western Isles,' he announced loudly.

The steward examined the proffered emblem carefully, then scratched the details in his ledger with a long quill.

'Welcome to Camelot.'

## Chapter Two

# Chapter Two

The Grand Tournament of Camelot was one of the most eagerly anticipated weeks of the year. From far and wide, from neighbouring kingdoms and from across distant seas, people had been steadily gathering for several weeks, the atmosphere gradually building to fever pitch.

Every night the taverns were full to bursting, the patrons arguing animatedly about which knight had the best chance of winning. Wagers were made, sides were taken and arguments often spilled out into the street in rowdy tangles, swiftly dispersed by the palace guards.

Each new knight who arrived was met by a sea of eager faces, cheering and shouting, and a steady stream of officials, sternly intent on ensuring that they were properly registered for the event. The walls of the castle were alive with pennants and flags from dozens of kingdoms, the banqueting halls and royal chambers ablaze with torches night after night as King Uther Pendragon greeted each arrival in turn.

Traders and salesmen of dozens of different nationalities had set up their stalls outside the castle walls, each jostling with the other for the custom of the excited crowds. For the inhabitants of Camelot and the villagers from the surrounding districts, it was a chance to buy goods and trinkets from far distant lands, to sample food and drink that they had never dreamed of. Trade was almost as important as the tournament itself.

Preparing the grand arena had kept the labourers and craftsmen of Camelot busy for weeks, flattening the earth on which the battles would play out and erecting the stands for the audience. Slowly the structure had taken shape in the field outside the castle gates, the labourers watched day after day by excited, eager children. Positioned on one side of the stands was the scoreboard – a tall wooden frame studded with pegs on which the colours of the competing knights would be hung, only to be removed one by one as knights were defeated, the victors being moved up to the next tier.

On the other side of the arena another field had been designated as a preparation area for the competing knights; a low stable building had been converted into a temporary armoury and there were small tents for each competitor. Camelot's tournament was popular because of the simplicity of its premise: the challenge was simply knight versus knight, on foot, hand-to-hand, with the ancient weapons of battle, the sword and scimitar, blade against blade. It was the way that Uther Pendragon liked it: battle stripped down to its most basic level, a simple test of strength and skill, not dressed up in any way. It made the tournament brutal and dangerous, and the victory all the more desirable.

Over the years Camelot's tournament had become increasingly popular, drawing more and more knights to the kingdom to compete. This year there were enough entrants to keep the crowds entertained for nearly a week and each of the arrivals had one goal – to be proclaimed the overall champion.

Blacksmiths had been toiling well into the evenings to ensure that no knight would be without a weapon come the day, and smithy walls were heavy with gleaming swords and shining armour, while servants hurried to and fro collecting spare weapons constructed to their master's unique specifications. The fights put great strain on the sword blades, and no one wanted to be left with inferior weapons on the day.

Many of the older boys of the lower town had been

recruited as servants for the occasion. For weeks now they had been schooled in the rules of the tournament and the duties that the visiting knights would expect them to fulfil. Almost all would be placed with those visiting knights who were unable to bring their own entourage with them, whilst an unlucky few would be held back in the eventuality of sickness amongst the servants to Camelot's own knights.

There was intense rivalry amongst the boys, each of them wearing the emblem of their allocated knight like a badge of honour. For them, failure in their duties was tantamount to failure in the arena.

After the knights of Camelot, it was the eastern knights who had the greatest following. With their curved swords and richly decorated tunics and cloaks, they seemed exotic and mysterious and to be placed in their service was considered a great honour.

The highest honour, however, was to be awarded the role of servant to the reigning champion, a task given even more importance this year because the current champion was Uther Pendragon's own son, Prince Arthur. Amongst the servants, it had been a source of angry conversation and bitter disappointment that Arthur's latest servant was hardly ideal for the position.

★

The morning sun had just cleared the treetops, bathing the walls of Camelot in soft yellow light. Arthur Pendragon stood tall in the training fields, stretching and feeling the warmth of the sun on his back. The air was filled with the sound of sword blades clashing and the bellows of the knights as they practised. The noise gave Arthur goose bumps, though he wasn't sure if that was excitement at the thought of the impending tournament or apprehension at the expectations of the court.

He had had to sit through another of his father's speeches about honour and chivalry again at breakfast, of the role of the knight, and how the reputation of the royal name of Pendragon would rest upon his shoulders in the coming days. It had not put Arthur in the best of moods.

His mood became sourer as his sparring partner emerged from inside the castle.

Merlin.

Arthur felt himself flush with anger and embarrassment. Of all the people who could have been placed as his servant, Merlin was the absolute worst. And at such a vital time too! He had tried to talk his father out of it, but Uther Pendragon was having none of it. In his eyes

Merlin had already proved himself by saving his son's life from the treachery of an evil witch; placing him at Arthur's side was right and proper.

Arthur twirled his sword angrily. He still wasn't sure quite how Merlin had managed to engineer matters so that he had looked so heroic, but Arthur was certain of one thing – he was going to make Merlin regret every day spent in his service.

Merlin staggered out onto the fields, his lanky frame weighed down by the training armour that he had been supplied with. He tugged at the front of the ill-fitting breastplate. Arthur's previous servant had been considerably wider in girth, and even though Merlin had pulled the straps as tight as they would go, the armour still hung off him. He really wasn't sure how much protection it was going to give him; at the moment it just seemed to be sliding around every time he moved.

He stared across at where Arthur Pendragon twirled his sword in the early morning light. Arthur was determined to get in as much practice as he could before tomorrow. Unfortunately, practice meant that he had to have someone to practise *with*, and with all the other knights and servants concentrating on their own tournament strategies, that someone was Merlin.

The prince's sword stabbed down into the hard earth and Arthur leaned on the hilt, peering at Merlin.

'Ready?'

Merlin gave a nervous smile. 'Would it make any difference if I said no?'

Arthur shook his head. 'Not really.'

Merlin barely had time to slip the oversized helmet onto his head and raise his shield before Arthur swung his sword in a wide arc. Merlin could feel vibrations shudder through his entire body as the blow connected.

With each swing of his sword Arthur called out, trying to get Merlin to parry.

'Shield! Body! Shield!'

Merlin flailed wildly with his shield as blow after blow rained down on him.

'Body! Shield!' cried Arthur. 'Come on, I've got a tournament to win! You're not even *trying*!'

Merlin staggered backwards, vainly trying to ward off blows, but the sword was so heavy he could barely lift it and the huge helmet kept sliding down over his eyes, obscuring Arthur from view.

'Helmet!'

A sudden blow to the side of his head sent him reeling one way. Before he could even regain his balance, another blow to the other side of his helmet sent him staggering back the other way. His foot slipped on the dew-soaked grass and he toppled backwards with a crash, his helmet rolling away.

As Merlin lay on his back staring at the blue of the sky and wondering why everything seemed to be swirling, Arthur's face loomed over him, nodding approvingly, Merlin's mood clearly brightened by Merlin's demonstration of his skill.

'You're braver than you look. Most servants collapse after the first few blows.'

'Oh, great. That's good to know.' Merlin tried to focus, shaking his head to try and clear the ringing. 'So, is it over?'

Arthur gave a sly smile. 'That was just the warm-up.' He held up a spiked ball on a long chain. 'How's your mace work coming along?'

Merlin let his head thump back onto the grass. He was never to going to survive until lunch time.

Arthur watched as Merlin staggered back to his feet and went to retrieve his helmet. Despite himself the prince had to admit that he was surprised at how well Merlin had stood up to the bout. Arthur had been unnecessarily hard on him, fully expecting him to be out for the count after the first few blows. Not only had Merlin taken the beating without complaint, but he was actually prepared to carry on. Perhaps he wasn't the total waste of space that he had at first seemed to be.

Groaning, Merlin bent down and picked up the battered and dented helmet. With a resigned look over at Arthur, he slipped the helmet back onto his head and hefted the shield onto his arm.

Arthur raised his mace.

'Let's see how long you can keep going this time,' he murmured.

Merlin stumbled down the long, flagstoned corridor of the servants' quarters. All around him people bustled to and fro with plates piled high with food prepared for the next day's tournament feast. The air was full of the smells of roasting meats, spiced ales and baking breads.

At the end of the corridor was a steep, narrow spiral staircase. A sign hanging on the wall read: *Court Physician*. Merlin climbed the stairs, wincing at every step. At the top was a heavy wooden door. He pushed it open and stumbled gratefully into the musty, cinnamon-scented calm of Gaius' chambers.

The room was large and gloomy, lit by shafts of light that lanced down from windows high in the curving stone walls and by dozens of torches dotted around the place. Bookcases and cupboards were squeezed into every alcove, each one bulging under the weight of books and bottles. A low bed was tucked against a far wall.

Gaius was huddled over the huge wooden table that dominated the room, decanting drops of vivid purple liquid into a collection of large glass bottles. He was an old man, his long grey hair hanging in unruly strands over his simple robes. He looked up as Merlin entered.

'So, how was your first day as Arthur's servant?' he asked.

Merlin squinted at him, tapping the side of his head with the palm of his hand.

'Can you hear clanging?' he said as he tried to flatten his hair which was sticking out wildly from his head. He wasn't sure if he would ever hear anything other than ringing in his ears for the rest of his life. His breastplate had slipped so that it was hanging down over his waist and somehow he'd managed to get one of his leg shields twisted around so that it was facing the wrong way.

Gaius got up and guided Merlin to one of the low stools that dotted the room. Merlin groaned as the old physician started to rub at the knots in his aching shoulders.

'I'm certain that it couldn't have been that bad,' said Gaius.

'It was horrible!' protested Merlin. 'No, it was worse than horrible. *Merlin, do this, Merlin, do that, Merlin, stand there whilst I whack you around the head with a sword.*'

Gaius grimaced. He had tended to several of Arthur's servants in the past and knew the damage that these 'practice' bouts could inflict. The difference was that Arthur's previous servant, Morris, had been considerably sturdier than Merlin, and even he had ended up in the physician's chambers on more than one occasion. He would have to stock up on his healing balms and ointments.

'Sounds painful.'

'Trust me! It was! I haven't stopped running around all day and I've still got to learn all about tournament etiquette by tomorrow morning.'

Merlin glanced across at a large leather-bound tome lying at the far end of the table. From amongst the hundreds of books that lined the walls of Gaius' chambers, he had found a book about the duties expected of a knight's manservant, and the rules and regulations of a tournament.

Well, perhaps *found* wasn't quite the right word, but then it was hardly his fault if Gaius' filing system was less than efficient. It would have taken hours, perhaps even days, of searching if he hadn't made use of his rather special talents.

He stretched out his hand towards the book and muttered a series of harsh, alien words under his breath, feeling the familiar warmth building in his head. His eyes flared with a glittering, golden glow and the book slid across the table towards him, pages flipping open to the place where Merlin had been reading over breakfast. The page showed a diagram of a knight's armour.

Exasperated, Gaius clouted him hard across the back of the head.

'What have I told you about using magic like that?'

Merlin winced. He knew that the old physician was right. He felt safe in Gaius' rooms, and that was making him careless. 'If I could actually feel my arms then I'd pick up the book myself!' he complained.

'Never mind your arms.' Gaius glared at him. 'What am I going to do if you get caught?'

Merlin glanced up at him, a quizzical eyebrow raised. 'What *would* you do?'

The two stared at each other for a moment, both well aware of the consequences if Uther Pendragon ever learned that sorcery was being practised within the walls of Camelot, let alone what he would do if he discovered that a young sorcerer was actually living under his protection. On his first day in Camelot, Merlin had seen for himself the fate awaiting anyone using magic. He felt a knot in the pit of his stomach as he remembered the dull thud that the executioner's axe had made as it fell.

'You just make sure that it doesn't happen,' said Gaius sternly. 'For both our sakes.'

Merlin nodded and picked up the book, trying to shake the unpleasant image of the execution from his mind. There were pages of rules and regulations that he was meant to memorize, and details of the duties that he was meant to perform. It was complicated. Confusing.

And dull.

He slumped back in his chair, letting the book thump down onto the table.

'I save Arthur from being killed and I end up as his servant. How is that fair?'

Gaius shrugged. It was true that without Merlin's in- tervention Arthur would have met an unpleasant end at the hands of a witch, Mary Collins, but to have revealed the true extent of Merlin's involvement would have meant exposing his magical abilities. Besides, as far as Uther was concerned, awarding Merlin the position of Arthur's manservant was a great honour.

'I'm not sure that fairness comes into it.' Gaius gave Merlin's arm a sharp tug, stretching the muscles. 'You never know, it might be fun.'

Merlin gasped with pain and looked up at him in disbelief. 'You think that mucking out Arthur's horses is going to be fun? You should see my list of duties!'

Gaius shrugged. 'We all have duties. Even Arthur.'

'Oh, yeah.' Merlin gave a snort of contempt. 'It must be so tough for him. All the girls, and the glory, and the trophies. And more girls. Poor old Arthur.'

'He is the future king!' said Gaius impatiently. 'Everyone expects so much of him. He's under a lot of pressure.'

Merlin winced as Gaius gave his aching shoulder another squeeze. 'That makes two of us!'